Pc

John and Ann

With ...

Stephen.

Postcard from the Common
Stephen Lewis

YouCaxton Publications
Oxford & Shrewsbury

ISBN 978-1-912419-88-3
Printed and bound in Great Britain.

Published by YouCaxton Publications 2019
YCBN: 01

YouCaxton Publications

enquiries@youcaxton.co.uk

To Lucy

and in memory of my parents
Marjorie and Clement Lewis

"There are four kinds of loss. There is the loss of beauty, especially that exquisite beauty of the small and complex and unexpected, of frog-orchids or sundews or dragonflies. There is the loss of freedom, of highways and open spaces, which results from the English attitude to land-ownership.... There is the loss of historic vegetation and wildlife, most of which once lost is gone for ever. ... I am specially concerned with the loss of meaning. The landscape is a record of our roots and the growth of civilization. Each individual historic wood, heath, etc. is uniquely different from every other, and each has something to tell us."

The History of the Countryside by Oliver Rackham

Phoenix 1986, pp.25 - 26

Contents

1.

Burning

Autumn 1944. A blindingly bright flash of light in the dark moonless night was quickly followed by the loud blast of an explosion. As Luke quickly got out of bed and drew back the curtains he knew straightaway what had happened, as he was used to the planes flying in low to land on the runway. From his bedroom window he could see the flames reaching beyond the tops of the trees in the wood. He put on his dressing gown and went towards his father's bedroom. His father was already out of bed still in his pyjamas and they met on the landing.

"A plane's come down on the common and it's on fire. You stay here and go back to bed, it's no place for an eight year old, and I'll go." With that his father ran downstairs, put on his coat and vanished out of the back door. Luke waited for a few seconds then put on his coat and his shoes and followed his father outside, keeping a safe distance.

The house Luke and his father lived in was situated on the edge of the common which had been turned into an airfield at the start of the war. To get to the fire, which Luke could see was now burning fiercely, he had to cross the road in front of the house, carefully crawl through the airfield's perimeter barbed wire fence using a piece of material snagged on the fence to protect his fingers and onto the heathland of the common. He could see the fire burning brightly on the edge of a small group of trees, some way off the runway, and he was there in less than a minute.

Luke knew he had to keep himself hidden from his father, so he stayed in amongst the trees. He heard the airfield's fire engine and an ambulance approaching, and he could see his father standing nearby to help once they arrived. The heat from the fire on his face made him grimace, and, as the brightness of the fire lit up everything around, he crouched down on the woodland floor so as not to be seen, half hidden behind the trunk of an oak tree. He saw the frame of the aircraft, one of the large bombers that were used to train pilots to prepare them for night-time bombing raids. At the front of the plane he could see that someone was struggling to get out, clearly the pilot. He was flailing around, and it looked to Luke as if he couldn't open the window of the cockpit to get out. The flames were by now all over the plane, and even inside the cockpit. The man continued to try to get out, but Luke could only watch, frozen by shock, gazing on a scene the like of which he had never witnessed before. And the heat was getting more intense. The man eventually managed to smash the widow of the cockpit, clambered out of the aircraft, jumped and fell onto the ground. Not only his clothing but also his face was on fire. He still had his pilot's goggles on but he clearly found it difficult to open his eyes in the blinding heat, and he tried frantically to put out the flames with his hands. He started to stagger forwards to where Luke was in the trees, limping as if he had injured one of his legs as well, with his arms open as if gesturing to him, shaking violently and screaming in agony. Luke remained paralysed with fear although he knew he should try and help him. The man collapsed on the ground. Soon the firemen arrived and started to douse the man with water, and Luke's father ran up to him, took off his coat and tried to cover him with it to put out the flames. Other firemen were busy getting the hoses unwound, coupling one length to another and putting the far end into the pond at the edge of the wood to put out the flames on the plane. The fire was quickly put out, and Luke's father tried to comfort the man before the ambulance men arrived and took him away on a stretcher, still screaming in agony. Luke could hear voices saying that the other members of the crew had been able to parachute safely before the crash, but it looked like the pilot had decided to try and land the plane.

Luke knew he had to get home before his father, so he crawled through the trees as silently as possible and ran home, going a different way. He didn't sleep that night.

The next morning they both came downstairs for breakfast in the kitchen, a meal of toast and jam with mugs of sugared tea. Luke made the toast whilst his father brewed the tea, placing the teapot on a stand on the kitchen table and covering it with a tea cosy made to look like a country cottage. With tea, sugar, butter and jam strictly rationed they had to limit themselves to what they could eat and drink. The kitchen table itself was wooden and covered with a plastic tablecloth, with three chairs. Luke asked his father, as innocently as he could, what had happened, and his father replied:

"A bomber came down on the common by the copse, losing control when it was coming into land. It's not clear why it crashed, but it careered into the heather, narrowly missing the trees, and caught fire."

"Did all the crew manage to get out?"

"Yes they all managed to get out safely before it crashed as they said the pilot told them to bale out and use their parachutes, apart from one unlucky chap, the pilot himself, who for some reason could not get out of the plane after it crashed. He managed to get out eventually, but he was badly burnt and he was taken to the hospital."

"How is he?"

"I'll find out later today. I don't think it's looking good for him."

"Did you know him?" asked Luke.

His father paused before saying "That's enough questions. Finish your toast and then it's time to get your boots on and let those chickens and geese out."

And this time Luke did what he was told.

2.

Hidden in Sand

1951. Seven years later. The war was over and the airfield was closed. The planes and the men and women who had worked on the airfield were gone. All that remained were the runways, the perimeter road, the control tower, the hangars and the buildings used to accommodate the airfield personnel, which all soon became derelict. The memories of what the place was, and what it represented, had started to fade. There were no doors in the buildings or glass in the windows, and graffiti began to appear on the walls. The runway which once saw large bomber planes thundering along as they took off had now become a place for local people to learn how to drive a car before taking their driving test.

The life of the common returned as much as it could to how it was before the airfield was built. Luke's father was no longer employed as ground crew at the airfield, and he started to exercise his commoners' rights again by putting five cattle out onto the common to graze. He took odd jobs locally using the mechanical and metal working skills he had learnt from his time at the airfield. Repairing farming equipment was his speciality. Luke was now fifteen years old. He always helped his father by tending the cattle and bringing them in to be milked in the morning before school. His father used to do the milking by hand, although they could easily have purchased some milking equipment, as he enjoyed it as part of the daily routine. The only equipment he used was a three-legged milking stool and some buckets. Sometimes the cattle would move about whilst being milked, and he could get injured by a flick of a tail or a sudden jerk of the head, as the horns of the cattle were not cut off. Afterwards he would pour the milk into a churn and put it beside the road for collection, keeping back just enough for their needs. Luke also used to herd the cattle round to different parts of the common during the weekends and school holidays. When it was hot and sunny he took them into a small group of trees, when it was windy he took them to shelter by the side of the old airfield control tower, and when the rain came down he would sometimes take them inside the tower. They stayed outside on the common throughout the year, even in the coldest of winters when snow covered the vegetation and Luke's father bought in some hay to feed them. Sometimes they would take one to market to be slaughtered. Luke looked after the cattle so attentively, giving them all names and getting to know their personalities, that at times his father chided him.

"Spending so much time with those cattle, you must know every square inch of the common by now."

When younger, Luke would run upstairs to his bedroom when his father teased him in this way and fling himself on his bed. He just loved being on the common, being in the open air, breathing the freshness of the day, even when the hard frosts came or the cold north wind blew. At the times when his father teased him he longed for his mother to put her arm around him tenderly and affectionately. But this would never happen again. His mother had died during the war, just a month before the plane crash.

Luke spent as much time as he could outside on the common. His spirits rose as soon as he felt the grass beneath his feet. The heathers, the wildflowers and grasses on either side of the runway, large areas of the common that had been mown regularly to provide safe run-off for the aircraft, now were able to grow, flower and set seed. Rather than being a uniform green or brown, the common was able to regain its variety of colours, with different shades of green, yellow, pink and purple flowers in the spring and summer, and darker browner hues in the autumn and winter. Plants and shrubs of different heights were now able to flourish, and in other parts of the common tree seedlings and saplings were stretching up towards the light. The whole common looked scrubbier, less tidy and less manicured, more haphazard and unkempt.

The airfield had of course left its mark apart from the structures. Bulldozers had been used to construct the airfield so now the common was completely flat, and small hollows and wetter patches had been lost. Wide skies arched over the horizon, and the impression of space, stillness and quietness had returned, as if a large crowd had been making a big noise but had suddenly stopped its shouting.

But there was not complete silence. Birds were able to return to the common. From first light the song thrush pierced what remained of the night's darkness, repeating his short song two or three times. By early morning the skylark had taken to the wing, dropping his ceaseless song all over the common. Yellowhammers with their hesitant song, and willow warblers singing wistfully added their voices and colours to the scene. At dusk the strange sound of a churring nightjar could be heard, too well camouflaged to be seen during the day.

The flowers, leaves and seeds now provided a feast for the insects. Butterflies and moths found suitable areas to lay their eggs and, once they had hatched, the caterpillars found plenty of leaves to feed on, and they in turn provided sustenance for the birds. Beetles, black, brown and green, scuttled about the vegetation, and bees, yellow, black and white, found flowers yielding their sweet nectar. Wasps and spiders were able to seek out their insect prey. Rabbits returned to their old warrens now that more grass was available for them, providing food for stoats and weasels which hunted the rabbits both above and below the ground. Mice, voles and shrews increased in numbers, prey for the kestrels by day and the owls by night. Parts of the common had been left untouched by the airfield, where pockets of heather had continued to flourish. The pond continued to be a haven for dragonflies and the occasional moorhen or coot, and the woodland areas remained a home for the badgers. Trails through the grass were left by the foxes. The web of life, the infinite connections between all the plants and the creatures, had returned to the common like a sickly child given nourishment, light and air once more. Colours, sounds, smells and shapes were all coming back in abundance as the life of the common returned to how it had been for centuries before the war. And in midsummer small blue butterflies fluttered around the grasses and the crimson heathers. An elderly woman came to the common regularly, sometimes with her butterfly net when she would try to catch and examine the blue butterflies before releasing them. Sometimes she wondered round different parts of the common with her notebook just counting them, and at other times she came with another woman who had a sketchpad and a few paints and sat on a stool to paint the butterflies and the heath in watercolours.

In the summer Luke would spend all day on the common tending the cattle. Although they would eat some of the grass and the flowers, as there were only five of them there was more than enough for both the cattle and the wildlife to flourish. Luke's father was the only commoner who exercised his rights to graze the common. Other people who had the commoners rights attached to their properties near the common no longer bothered, although some would still take an interest in the common and wanted to see their rights preserved. Sometimes Luke wouldn't talk to anyone all day, other times he would meet some of the local people out for a walk on the common with a dog, or talk to the other commoners who were pleased that the old ways of grazing the common had not entirely died out. On occasions local boys out for a walk on the common would throw stones at him and his cattle, shouting obscenities and laughing as they goaded each other on. Luke didn't throw the stones back, but just tried to hide, and later when they were gone he might sit down and try to fight back the tears. Although he loved the common and being on the common, he didn't much care for the fact that he had to be on the common for such long periods of time, tending the cattle in all weathers.

He had one friend whom he saw often, a Polish girl a year older than him called Alina. Alina's family had been resettled in the old corrugated iron nissen huts which had been the living quarters for the airfield personnel next to the common, along with other Polish families. They came here after her father had served in the Polish army alongside the British in the war. The conditions were primitive, with several families sharing washrooms and toilets.

Alina liked being away from the resettlement camp, walking over the common, and when she met up with Luke she would enjoy telling him about her life in Poland before the war. At times when they had been younger they would play games, such as climbing a large, spreading tree near the boundary of the common, with one trying to catch the other without touching the ground. Or racing around the pond edge, or seeing who could climb onto the roof of the old airfield control tower first by using the drainpipes, the balcony and the empty windows. Or picking plantains in the grassland and knocking the flower heads off the stems. But most of the time they would just sit and talk about their very different lives. Alina would talk about what she wanted to do when she was older, saying she would want to be the best showjumper in the world with a stable full of horses, or maybe a dressage champion, as she loved having that sense of being in control. Luke was more modest, saying he would like to stay on the common, and look after his father when he was old and infirm. When they spoke they would sometimes be lying on their backs on the grass until one of them, usually Alina, would sit up and say what a load of nonsense they had been talking, and then they would play fight. Luke, for all his modesty, was a tough little fighter, and, especially when Alina riled him by calling him a motherless child, he would get angry and use his fists to hit Alina on her arms.

One day, as the heat of summer began to weaken with autumn drawing closer, when they were both in their mid-teens, they walked through the copse into the area where the airplane had crashed. The area had become overgrown with brambles which now in late summer bore a heavy crop of blackberries, and they both edged carefully into the centre of the bushes where the biggest fruits were to be found. Alina was eating them as she picked them, but Luke put the ones he picked into a bag to take them home later. The ground was sandy and full of rabbit holes, with mounds of sand where the rabbits had been digging their warrens. When Luke stepped on one of these he felt the sand give way and then he sensed that there was something under his foot. Leaning down he brushed some sand away and found a pen, an old fashioned fountain pen, and picked it up. The pen was green in colour with black marbling, and when he wiped it clean he saw that there was some writing along its length. He called to Alina to come over as he made his way out of the brambles.

"Take a look at this" he said as they both sat down on the grass. "It's got writing on it."

"Give it to me" said Alina in her usual forthright manner. Holding the pen lengthways she turned it round and held it close to her eyes.

"It's in gold, but I can't make it out. It looks as though it has been damaged in some way as well. You have a go."

Luke took the pen back and examined it carefully. "Some of the writing is missing. It begins with an F, and I can see a small t and then there is a gap and several other letters, one of which looks like a J, but all of them are difficult to make out."

"Whoever it belonged to must have been really careless to have dropped it. It looks like an expensive pen." said Alina.

Luke, still holding the pen, stayed silent for a few moments and lifted his eyes and looked around him. The colour drained from his cheeks and he felt a chill as he realised that they were sitting by the place where the aircraft had crashed, when he had seen the pilot stagger towards him in flames. He looked at the pen again and took a closer look at the damage. Could this have been the pilot's pen? Could the damage have been caused by the fire? Could the pen have dropped out of one of the pilot's pockets as he ran towards him? All too quickly a host of questions entered his head. He also wondered if he was putting two and two together and making five – perhaps it was nothing at all to do with the pilot.

He looked at Alina. He did not really know where to start, as he thought she would be pretty dismissive of any story he told her about the pilot. But he went ahead and told her all about the night the plane had crashed and what he had witnessed. How he had run across the common to see what had happened in the middle of the night, the fierceness of the heat from the fire, and the image that was still in his mind of the pilot running towards him, arms outstretched. He also told her what his father had told him the day after the crash, about the pilot dying in hospital. He was, however, completely wrong about Alina's response. After listening to what Luke told her, she said:

"I think it was the pilot's pen, and I think we should find out more about him. He was a hero, as was everyone who gave their lives to win the war. If it were not for people like him I would not be here now, and your life would probably be very different. We owe it to him to find out who he was and about his life … and his death."

Luke looked at the pen once more, twisting it round in his fingers. He was pleased, really pleased, with what Alina had said.

"Thanks Ally. I agree." Ally was what he called her when he felt close to her, rare moments when they were not bickering and teasing each other.

"But where do we start? I suppose it would help first if we could find out his name. I shall ask my Dad this evening as he knew a lot of people on the airfield."

When he arrived back home Luke went straight upstairs and lay on his bed. He took the pen out of his pocket and held it in his fingers once more. Although much of the gold lettering had disappeared, he could make out something more, especially after the J. It looked like there had been four more letters and then another word. Could it be his name? If so, what was the C at the start of the lettering, and could he also make out an A?

Luke went downstairs to meet his father, who was making their tea in the kitchen.

"Dad, you remember that man who was killed in the plane crash on the heath in the war?"

"What of it?" was his father's curt reply.

"Well, do you know his name?"

Luke's father kept silent for a while, carrying the teapot over to the table, before pulling up a chair and sitting down. He poured out two mugs of tea.

"He was a brave man, Luke. There was an enquiry into the crash afterwards, with statements from witnesses and the rest of the aircrew and so on, all of whom had survived. Apparently he stayed with his plane after everyone else had baled out, tried to land the plane on the runway but couldn't due to the damaged engine, and made sure it crash landed on the common rather than carrying on into the buildings where all the men were stationed. And he paid the price."

"But what was his name?" said Luke.

"I can't tell you that, it was a long time ago, and I forget things like that."

"But it's not that long ago. If you can't tell me who can?" persisted Luke.

"The enquiry was led by a chap called Flight Commander George Porter, as he was then. He lives at the end house on Furze Lane. He might be able to help you, but I can't. And I would rather you did not bring it up again as they were .... difficult times. Things happen and you just have to live with it. Nothing to be gained by opening up and talking about things like that. You just have to get on with it as best you can. What's it to you, any road?" Luke knew his father always preferred not to talk about or express his emotions, for whatever reason, so he was not surprised by this response. But he thought his father was being more defensive than usual.

"I would just like to know. I was there after the crash despite what you told me not to come, and I saw him running towards me, on fire. I keep seeing him when I lie awake at night. It's as if he has become part of me" said Luke.

"I still think you are better off not knowing" replied his father, and with that he served up two plates of beans on toast. "And besides, you should have stayed in your bed that night. It was no place for a youngster. If you keep having nightmares about it that's your fault."

"It's not nightmares, it's just that I see him as if it were yesterday, stumbling towards me on fire, and it keeps me awake. I try not to think about him but sometimes I can't help it, as if the memory is too strong. He must have been in agony."

"Enough. Time for you to get the cattle in for milking."

The next day Luke went to find Alina. It was a fine morning with weak sunshine lighting up the green grass and the deep crimson red of the heather. The camp where Alina lived with her parents was on the far side of the common, and it was divided into a number of sites, with Alina's family living in Site 9, Hut 10. The corrugated iron hut was painted black and had been altered by having a front door cut into the curved side, which was decorated with painted flowers on a white background. Luke knocked at the front door and it was answered by Alina's mother.

"Come in, come in." she said, stretching out her arm and putting it round Luke's shoulder and walking him into their kitchen. "I just been baking, so you come at right time, no. Alina, Alina, Luke is come."

Alina came into the room. "Hi. Come for some breakfast?"

Alina thought that Luke father rarely gave him a proper breakfast. Alina's mother produced cups of tea in fine bone china with saucers decorated with flowers, and a plate of still warm homemade biscuits sitting on a doily. Luke helped himself to several of the biscuits, with Alina asking him sarcastically why he didn't just eat the lot.

Alina's father had served in the Polish army in the war, fighting in Italy where he had been wounded. Later he was sent to a rehabilitation hospital and was then reunited with his family near the common. He found work on various farms in the area, mainly driving tractors as his wartime injuries prevented him from too much physical work. Alina's mother had made their home as much like their home back in Poland had been, and the fact that they were living alongside some of their compatriots made it easier for them to maintain a Polish way of life. A small chapel had been constructed, a shop sold Polish goods and all the families celebrated Polish customs and feast days. Learning to speak English had been an uphill struggle for Alina's parents, but Alina herself had found it quite easy to pick up at school. Her mother in particular found it difficult, and when speaking to Luke she often got in a muddle.

"Seems like the day not too bad yet" she said to Luke, who agreed politely.

Luke looked at Alina. "I thought we could go round and see somebody who might be able to tell us more about what we found yesterday."

"OK" replied Alina. They left, with Alina putting a couple of biscuits into her pocket.

As they crossed the common they saw a tall, gaunt elderly woman in a long skirt with a large net in one hand running across the heather. Luke and Alina looked at each other.

"There's the bug lady, chasing the butterflies." said Luke. As he spoke the woman stopped, looked round, frowning. Luke and Alina quickly moved on.

"What was that about?" asked Alina.

"She's here a lot" replied Luke, "but talks to nobody".

When they came to a bungalow at the end of Furze Lane just off the common Luke knocked at the door and it was opened by a man with a remarkable moustache.

Former Flight Commander George Porter lived in the bungalow with his wife Margaret, his children having left home and moved away, although they sometimes came to stay bringing their children. George loved to regale his grandchildren with stories about the war and the planes he flew, although they would tend to fall asleep on his lap. He felt it was important that the story of those times, when the country was threatened with being invaded, was passed on to the younger generation. Margaret would often gently rebuke him for boring the grandchildren with tales of the past, especially if she knew they would much rather be outside playing. She had bought them small bicycles so that they could race up and down the old runways on the common. After the war he had stayed in the RAF for a few years before he retired, and came back to live by the common, which held so many memories for him. He would sometimes walk along the old runways and in his mind would hear the thundering sound of the bombers as they gathered speed for take-off.

"Yes?" the man said.

"Mr Porter?" asked Luke

"Yes" the man replied.

Luke produced the pen out of his pocket.

"We found this yesterday on the common where one of the airplanes crashed in the war. We think it may have belonged to one of the pilots. It's got some writing on it."

The man took the pen, looked at it carefully, and invited them into his lounge. On the walls of the room were paintings of wartime airplanes, and on the middle of a coffee table was a plate of ginger biscuits. Alina eyed Luke and shook her head, discouraging him from helping himself to yet more biscuits. Margaret, the Flight Commander's wife, entered the room and welcomed the two teenagers. "Would you like a cup of tea – the kettle's just boiled?" she asked.

"Yes please" replied Luke, and Margaret left the room.

"Now then, what do you want to know?" said the former Flight Commander, stroking his moustache. Alina had to give Luke a dig in the ribs with her elbow due to his shyness before he started to speak.

"I saw the plane that crashed on the common and caught fire when I was younger. Yesterday we found this pen at the place where it crashed, and we wondered if it belonged to the pilot, and what was his name was."

"You must have been a very young man when that happened. How old were you, and how come your parents allowed you to witness the crash?"

"I was eight, and my Dad told me to stay in bed, but I managed to sneak out when I heard the crash and saw the flames."

"Hmm. It was a terrible business." The Flight Commander paused before picking up the pen which Luke had placed on the table. "Yes, I think it was his. His name was Jim Craig. Flight Lieutenant Jim Craig. He was a fine pilot, came from Scotland."

Alina looked at Luke, elbowed him in the ribs and whispered "Go on" to him.

"Why did the plane crash, and why did the pilot die, and why didn't he escape like the others?" asked Luke, not looking at the Flight Commander, reciting a series of questions he had prepared in his head all at once, and then thinking that he might have been too direct.

The former Flight Commander took a deep breath and looked around him. He took out a pipe from his jacket pocket and filled it with tobacco.

"It was a while ago now, but I still recall the shock and sadness so many of our colleagues felt about what happened, and the investigation which I was asked to conduct. Firstly there was a long form to fill in within four days of the crash, followed by a Court of Inquiry which I led. That meant interviewing everyone who was connected with the incident and the plane to try to establish exactly what had happened and what lessons could be learnt." He stopped, partly to think carefully his choice of words. He felt in his pocket for some matches and then lit his pipe and drew on it a couple of times. He liked talking about the war to younger people, although this incident was clearly somewhat difficult for him. His wife arrived back carrying a tray with fine bone china cups and saucers, as well as a teapot with a cosy, and started pouring out the tea.

"Help yourselves to sugar" she said, and Luke and Alina took three spoonfuls each, despite the fact that rationing was still in force. The Flight Commander did not have any tea, and resumed what he was saying.

"Now, you have to understand that the planes that were used at the airfield were for training pilots and were not the best. Many were what we called war weary, that is to say they had completed many hours flying in bombing raids over enemy territory but were no longer deemed fit to continue, and they were generally in poor condition. So they were farmed out to training airfields like this one to help train pilots and crew. Some had been badly damaged, but they were all that

2. Hidden in Sand

we had got. The country was fighting a war, and threatened with invasion, so we had to make the best of it. This particular aircraft was a twin engine bomber, known popularly as a flying coffin, not only because it was accident prone but also because of its shape. What we found in the investigation was that one of the plane's engines had failed mechanically and had burst into flames, setting the fuselage alight before the plane crash landed. The plane, which had been coming in to land anyway, began to descend rapidly, and with just one engine remaining it would have been extremely difficult to control at all. The crew had managed to get out and parachute safely when told by the pilot to bail out at the time the fire took hold, without any serious injury. The pilot was clearly having difficulty controlling the plane and it seemed to be heading for the staff living quarters at the edge of the common. He managed to divert it, however, and crash landed on the common well away from the runway and the living quarters. If he had bailed out sooner and left the plane to crash the likelihood was that the living quarters would have been hit, and there would have been many more casualties

"The pilot, however, was not as lucky as his crew, as for some reason he was unable or unwilling to disembark, and he was still in the plane when it crash landed, and it seemed for a while afterwards. He sustained a bad gash on his forehead as a result of the impact and was not able to get out straightaway, he may have been unconscious for a while. Some people said that maybe the cockpit window did not open properly and he struggled to get out, and we did find a fault with this on inspection. By the time he did get out his clothes were on fire. Despite everyone's efforts to save him he died the following day from extensive burns in the hospital." He paused briefly, composing himself. "It was such a dreadfully painful way to die. He must have been in agony. The whole unit was in shock for days afterwards as he was so widely liked, we were all so close, it was as if we had lost a member of our family. There really ought to be a memorial to him on the common, and to others from the airfield who were killed in the war whilst serving our country."

"So why was the window faulty?" asked Alina.

The Flight Commander paused. "Nobody knows." He paused again. "He was a good man, very popular in the area whilst he was based here. He spent a lot of time on the common when he was not on duty. Local people will tell you more about him."

At this point his wife interrupted. "I hope he's not boring you with his wartime tales in the way he bores the grandkiddies. Sometimes I think he is still living in the war."

"No, not a bit. We really like listening to what he has got to tell us" replied Luke.

"They were asking about one of the pilots who lost his life on the airfield. It's good to see that people are still interested in what happened" said the Flight Commander.

Alina and Luke thanked Mr and Mrs Porter and left. As they walked back across the common Alina spoke to Luke.

"I suppose you still want to find out more about your war hero."

"He's not a war hero" snapped Luke.

"He certainly has made a mark on you though."

After a pause Luke said they should find someone else who could tell them about Jim Craig. They parted, Alina to return home and Luke to see to the cattle.

When Luke arrived home his father quizzed him.

"Well, did you find out what you wanted?"

"Sort of" replied Luke, as he went past his father and up to his bedroom. He lay on his bed, and picked up the fountain pen. The writing and the spacing between the surviving letters now made some sense. Flight Lieutenant James Craig, it read, not Jim Craig. With his title on one line and the name underneath. He put the pen down. Questions were turning round in his head, with little by way of answers. Why did the pilot get stuck? Was it the window that was the problem or was it something else? If it was a fault with the window why did it happen? And why did the engine fail in the first place? And why did the pilot look at him in the eyes as he ran away from the burning plane? The Flight Commander said that he was a popular man, but what did this mean? Before long he fell asleep.

The next morning at breakfast, after Luke had told his father the pilot's name, he asked if he had known him.

"Jim Craig? I knew him as well as anyone, I suppose. Many people knew him, as on his time off he was often to be seen on the common. But I can't tell you much about him"

Can't or won't, thought Luke.

"Is there anyone who could tell me more about him?"

"You'll have to find that out for yourself."

Luke sensed he was not going to get anything more out of his father, so he left without another word and walked out onto the common. The cattle had wandered towards the pond where they were drinking. He found Alina by the pond, watching the dragonflies restlessly flying around and the swallows swooping down to pick insects off the surface of the water.

"So have you thought any more about your war hero?" she asked.

"I need to speak to people to find out more about him. Apparently a lot of people knew him. I think the best person to visit would be Bill Westwood – he knows everything about everybody. Lived here all his life, and people say he was born on the common."

"You mean his mother actually gave birth to him here, in the open air? That's ridiculous" said Alina.

"That's what people say".

As they walked across the common they collected some dead wood lying on the ground. Luke knew that Mr Westwood had commoners' rights to collect dead wood for his fire and thought he would appreciate some sticks. Mr Westwood's home was far from a conventional house, more like a small cabin. There was no knocker on the door, and so Luke knocked on the door panel, which immediately fell inside.

"You idiot" said Alina, as a voice could be heard from within.

"What's up" said the voice, as two dogs began barking. Mr Westwood came to the door and looked through where the panel had been. "Is that young Luke? Who's that with you?"

"This is Alina. She lives in the camp on the other side of the common."

"So, a girlfriend then Luke."

"I think not" muttered Alina under her breath as she smiled at Mr Westwood.

"Well, you can't stand outside all day, you'd better come in. Is that wood for me? Thanks for that." Luke passed the branches through the door where the panel had been.

Bill Westwood had never married and always lived by himself, although he had enjoyed close friendships with a number of women. He wore a check shirt and an old tweed jacket, with a pair of corduroy trousers done up with baler twine around his waist. He wore no socks, just a pair of slippers. His home lacked the finer comforts that perhaps a wife would have given it, being quite sparse, but he liked it as it was. His life had always been centred on the common, and he used to let his two ponies out to graze there in the summer months. When he was younger he had worked in the building trade for much of the time. His voice was gravelly and harsh, as he was not often seen without a thin rolled-up cigarette between his lips.

"Don't you worry about that, I'll fix it later" said Mr Westwood.

He showed them into a room with bare floorboards, walls bedecked with horse brasses, bridles, old Christmas cards with pictures of birds, a couple of plates on the walls and wallpaper stained by years of tobacco smoke. As well as the wallpaper, his fingers and his teeth, none of which were straight, were all

2. Hidden in Sand

stained yellow from cigarette smoking during all of his adult life.

"Now then, what can I do for you? Sit yourselves down where you can find somewhere."

Alina and Luke sat down, or rather sunk down, on an old dishevelled settee which had one of its springs showing through the fabric. Mr Westwood sat on an upturned milk bottle crate.

"Well" said Luke hesitatingly, "We wondered…"

"You wondered" interrupted Alina.

"I wondered if you had known a pilot during the war who was stationed here called Jim Craig.

"Oh him. Yes I knew him. Why on earth would you want to know about him?"

"Just curious" replied Luke, unconvincingly, "I know he died here after his plane crashed."

Bill Westwood took out a small packet of tobacco and a cigarette paper, rolled a cigarette, lit it and drew so heavily on it that nearly half disappeared at once. The smoke stayed inside him for a while before he let it out. He then coughed, and put his fingers to his lips to remove a piece of tobacco before he spoke again, with the rasp of a heavy smoker.

"I knew him well, he was a good man, unlike some of the bastards round here. He would come round here on his days off with his bag of baccy, as he smoked a pipe, as many of them did. He would talk all about the common, the wildlife and the birds he saw on those parts that were not part of the airfield. Skylarks in particular was his thing, he used to walk round trying to find any nests on the ground, and, if he found one, he would tell me how many eggs were in it and how they were coloured, brown with black freckles he used to say. He was very knowledgeable about all of that. And he knew all the local ladies as well. Now tell me really why you are interested in him. Would you both like a cuppa?"

Alina and Luke both declined, but Mr Westwood got up and made himself a cup of coffee from a kettle that sat on top of his stove. He sat down again, topped up his cup of coffee from a bottle of whisky he kept by his chair and gulped down a mouthful.

"Let me show you this" said Mr Westwood, getting hold of a small photograph in a brass frame that rested on a window sill. "They were my parents, right good people too. They used to keep cattle on the common, just like you and your father do today. It's a pity more commoners don't do it now. In those days people kept their animals on the common, those with the rights attached to the title deeds of their properties. Everyone knew how many cattle, sheep, goats or whatever they were allowed to put out, so it was all clear. If anyone overstepped their mark the others soon sorted it out. Me, I'm too old for it now, but some of these young 'uns who have the commoners' rights are just not interested. They all want to spend all day in offices or whatever, rather than the fresh air in all weathers. Some say you can't blame 'em, it can be hard looking after stock on the common in the winters. So more power to you I say, and make sure you keep going. What will you be doing when you're grown up? Suppose you don't know yet, but think about it. With the common it will be a case of use it or lose it."

Luke told him about seeing the pilot on fire.

"I remember hearing about the crash, and the report which said that it was an accident as the plane was basically knackered. Mind you, he had some enemies, he did. Not just because he liked the company of women. The fact that he loved the common didn't go down well with some of the locals."

"Why was that?"

"You should go and talk to some of them to find out. Start with old boy Hughes at Orchard Farm, he should be able to tell you a thing or two. I had nothing against him, the pilot, mind, he was a thoroughly decent sort, the sort of bloke you could spend an afternoon with in the company of my good friend here" he said, reaching down and patting the bottle of whisky.

When they left and returned to sit by the pond on the common Alina turned to Luke and said: "So, maybe he was not a hero in some people's eyes."

"So what?" replied Luke, becoming embarrassed.

"And why are people saying that I am your girlfriend? Have you been putting round some gossip? Is it because you are a motherless child, eager to find some sort of replacement?"

"Shut up" said Luke, becoming angry. "What are you trying to say?"

"Luke, you've never told me how or why your mother died."

"I don't want to. It hurts."

"If you don't, the pain will never be easier for you. It may be hard but you have to try."

"I only know what my father told me. Apparently she had felt unwell one day due to some sort of infection. She died a few days later in the evening in hospital, despite the doctors doing all they could for her. It must have been a very bad infection. I think she knew she was dying, and I can remember sitting on her bed and holding her hand, and she drew me towards her to kiss me...." Tears came to Luke's eyes. "It all happened so quickly, I just could not understand that she was not going to get out of bed and be her normal self again. I can recall standing by the door of our cottage as the ambulance people carried her out on a stretcher. After she was dead she was placed back in her bed and people came round to see her, and then they put her in a coffin. The funeral was held in the local church, but I was just in a daze and I can't remember anything about it. She's buried in the graveyard there. It was only afterwards that I began to understand that she was not going to come back, that she had died and that life would never be the same again. It all happened just a few weeks before the pilot was killed in the crash. That's all I know. I have lots of memories of her, all happy ones. She was my Mum, and I loved her very much, and still do even though she has gone. Dad has put away all the photographs of her, as if he can't bear to be reminded of her. He refuses to speak about her, and gets cross if I mention her."

"Come on" said Alina in her usual matter-of-fact way, getting to her feet. "I've got to go back home."

The next day Luke went to meet Alina at her house. As he approached he could hear voices being raised in Polish, which stopped when he knocked on the door. Alina answered the door, grabbed her coat and stepped outside.

"What was all that about? queried Luke.

"Just the usual stuff, parents trying to lead your life for you. They want me to go to Poland."

"Why?"

"Well, they are worried that I will lose my Polishness, whatever that is. They think the longer I spend here without staying with relatives in Poland the less I am going to be interested in keeping up Polish traditions, speaking the mother tongue, reading books in Polish, listening to Polish music, eating Polish food and all that."

"And are you going to go?"

"Don't really want to, but my parents really want me to. I have never been back to Poland, I left when I was much younger, so I have no real idea what it's like."

"I don't want you to go" said Luke.

"Yes, but your opinion isn't worth a sackful of mushrooms!" replied Alina, laughing and prodding Luke in the ribs as she spoke.

After a pause Alina suggested they go and visit someone called old boy Hughes, as Mr Westwood had called him, who may be able to tell them more about the pilot.

"He lives on a farm just beyond the end of the old runway, so let's walk along there" said Luke.

They arrived at Mr and Mrs Hughes' house by opening a large pair of wrought iron gates and walking up a driveway past a shiny new car. They lived in a house that was larger than all the others that encircled the common as it had recently been extended and upgraded, and it was now a very grand farmhouse. Luke knocked at the door, but there was no reply apart from the loud barking of various dogs. They went round to the back of the house and spotted a man and a woman walking towards the house from the fields beyond.

"What do you want?" shouted the man from a distance.

"Hello." said Luke when they had come closer. "Are you Mr Hughes?

Mr Hughes looked up and replied: "I just might be. You're the young lad with the cattle on the common aren't you? And is that your girlfriend with you?"

Not again, thought Alina. "I am NOT his girlfriend" responded Alina hastily and firmly to ensure there was absolutely no confusion about this. "We're here to see if you can help us to find out more about one of the pilots who was killed on the airfield."

"Why in heaven's name do you want to know about that? Let's go indoors anyway" said Mr Hughes, "But first you'll have to let me take my boots off and then see to the dogs elsewise they'll have you for dinner."

Ken and Gillian Hughes's large farm had been in the family for several generations, and had increased in size when they had bought a neighbouring farm. It was now over three hundred acres, and they were very proud of what they had achieved over the years. During the war Italian prisoners-of-war had been billeted on the farm to help with the work, in particular growing and harvesting the crops, mainly potatoes and wheat. Crop yields were now at record levels, and they were keen to increase the yields still further, putting into practice any new farming methods as recommended by the government advisers.

They were not just farmers but business people too, and they concerned themselves with little else and did not spend much time conversing with other people in the area apart from about business matters. They ran the farm together, both of them having been brought up on farms.

"OK, coast is clear now" said Mrs Hughes after he had put the dogs in another room and closed the door, and they all entered the kitchen. Mrs Hughes went over to fill a kettle with water whilst Mr Hughes washed his hands in the sink. As they walked in Luke and Alina saw spread out on the table a large map. They looked at the map and recognised the outline of the common, the wooded areas, the heathland, the pond, the old runway. Luke pointed out where the plane had crashed. They also saw that some parts had been marked out with a blue crayon. Just then Mr Hughes entered with his wife, and he went over to the table and folded up the map and put it to one side.

"Now young Luke, what is it you want to know about a pilot that was killed on the airfield."

"I just want to know more about him. You see I heard the plane crash that night and went onto the common and saw him covered in flames. I've found out that his name was Jim Craig. Bill Westwood suggested that you might be able to tell us more about him."

"He made a lot of men here very jealous, including your Dad. Isn't that right Gill?" looking towards his wife.

"A lot of the womenfolk liked him" added Mrs Hughes. "But not me, I found him too nice. I prefer a man who is a bit more down to earth, a bit more business-like, less of the romantic type."

"What do you mean?"

"There was a lot of talk about him. You'll find out more sooner or later" said Mrs Hughes, adding "Ask your father."

Alina looked at Luke. She could see that he was genuinely confused and that he did not fully understand what was being implied.

"What else can you tell me?" asked Luke

"We didn't have that much to do with him, so nothing much. We knew he spent time on the common wandering about, not doing much if you ask me. Except that we've got work to do and it's time you two went back home." said Mr Hughes.

Alina decided to speak up. "Why is there a map of the common on the table?"

"It doesn't sound like you're from round here. Where are you from?" responded Mr Hughes.

"I live in the camp on the other side of the common. I'm Polish."

"Oh I see. So you think you can come round here asking a load of questions about things that don't concern you, young lady. You'd be better off keeping your Polish nose out of other people's business, not to say out of our country too. And as for you" looking at Luke "why on earth are you wasting your time looking after a few cattle on the common? Haven't you got anything better to do? Now push off the pair of you."

Once they were back outside they started walking back across the common, with Luke bowing his head, deep in thought. Alina prompted him.

"Come on Luke, young cattle herder, motherless child, what do you make of that?"

"I don't know. What was she trying to say? That my Dad isn't my real Dad, that the pilot was my Dad? That can't be right as I was born before the war started and the airfield was built."

"You'd better speak to your Dad about all that" replied Alina.

"Fat chance I'll get anything out of him. Don't much care for Mr and Mrs Hughes mind. Seemed to be wanting to plant a thought in my mind. And what did you make of what he said about you and your Polish nose?" said Luke, poking Alina's nose with his finger.

Alina smiled but said nothing. They continued walking across the common in silence. The skylarks were singing in their fluttering flight and the rabbits were nibbling the grassy mounds. Patches of heather were flowering bright pink next to the vivid yellow of the gorse. But none of this lifted their mood. When they reached Alina's home they parted.

"Don't bother coming round tomorrow, I've got other plans." said Alina.

Luke didn't respond but just carried on walking with his head bowed until he reached his home. His father was outside tending his vegetable patch with a hoe when he arrived. Luke stopped a short distance from his father and stared at him. He couldn't utter any words because as soon as he was about to say something a contradictory impulse or thought came into his head. How could he broach a subject that he knew his father didn't want to discuss? His father had his back turned towards Luke whilst he was hoeing, but eventually he turned round.

"Ah, there you are. Where are those cattle now that you're meant to be looking after?"

Luke knew he had been neglecting his livestock duties and fumbled for an answer.

"They're OK I suppose." he replied.

"Suppose isn't good enough. You'd better go and mind them if you want some supper."

With that Luke went to find the cattle.

3.

More Questions than Answers

Alina thought about what she and Luke had learnt about the pilot. She knew that Luke was finding it very difficult, that he was struggling to deal with what people were telling him. She also sensed that people were being evasive when they spoke to Luke, not giving him the full story, for whatever reason. Maybe it was because they did not want to see Luke hurt, maybe because they did not like talking about the war themselves, or maybe because they were trying to hide something.

She thought particularly about the Flight Commander. Perhaps he was not as open with Luke as he might have been. It had been as if he had felt uncomfortable in talking to Luke, that he had paused often when speaking as if he had to chose carefully what he said, and that he had ended the conversation sooner than he might have done. She decided to go and see him again, this time on her own.

When she arrived the Flight Commander answered the door and paused for a moment.

"Where's your friend?"

"I thought it would be best if I came on my own."

"You'd better come in I suppose." The Flight Commander took her into the lounge.

"Well, what is it this time?"

"You know the pilot that was killed that you told us about. Well, I don't really know how to put this, but is there anything else you can tell me?"

The Flight Commander took a deep breath.

"How well do you know Luke?" he asked.

"I've known him ever since I came to live here. We've always spent time together playing on the common and looking after his Dad's cattle."

"Well, I can tell you something, but I'd rather you kept it to yourself. Can you keep a secret, even from your boyfriend?"

"I can, but, honestly, he's not my boyfriend."

The Flight Commander stood up and walked across the room, thinking how best to say what he was going to say.

"When the crash was investigated one thing they had to look at was how well the aircraft was maintained. In this case it wasn't clear why the pilot didn't evacuate the plane sooner, but it was believed that for some reason he struggled to open the window once the plane had crash landed, which would have been his normal method of escape. By the time he managed to get it open it was too late, and he was on fire. So the investigators had to check who was responsible for the maintenance of the plane, not just the engine bit all the moving parts. Luke's father was a trained member of the ground crew on the airfield, and he had a lot of experience of farm machine maintenance as that was his job both before the war and since. You have to remember that this country was threatened with being invaded, so it was a case of all hands on deck. One of the people responsible for checking that aircraft on that day before it took off was Luke's father. It appeared that the window catch had become jammed for some reason, maybe it was faulty. The investigators interviewed him but no further action was taken. It was put down to mechanical error, with the engine failure in the first place and then the window failure which led to the pilot catching fire and his death."

Alina stayed silent.

"I hope you can understand why I could not tell this to Luke."

"I understand." said Alina, softly.

"Many people round here know what I have just told you but would not want to share it with Luke. Some of them will even put two and two together and think there may have been an element of foul play in what happened, but this was never proved, and I don't believe it myself."

A pause before the Flight Commander resumed speaking.

"Should Luke be told about this? I don't know. Will his father ever speak to him about it? I doubt it. What will you do with this information? That's up to you. You sensed there was something I did not tell you initially, you wanted to know what it was, and now you know what it was."

Alina rose from her chair, thanked him, shook him by the hand and left. She ran back home, with so many thoughts and questions swimming round her head.

Back at home she was just in time for tea and she sat down at the kitchen table, kissing her parents first.

"So where have you been this afternoon." asked her father.

"Been to see someone."

"You be careful going out and round on your own about here." said her mother. Her English was more broken than that of her husband, as she stayed at home a lot, cleaning, preparing meals or talking in her native tongue to other Polish people from the camp. Alina's father, meanwhile, was employed on local farms and used to talking with local people more, gaining a much better grasp of English.

"You know Luke" said Alina, changing the subject, and shrugging off her mother's comment as if to say she could look after herself. "How well do you know his Dad?"

Alina's mother responded. "Not many peoples round here know him that well. He keep himself to himself. We don't see most of him. But when we first was arrived here he was one of the few people who went out of their way in welcome us. Much people didn't bothered. They just either ignored us, or crossed over other side of road if we was going into the town. Some even shouted "Go back home" at us and some eggs and tomatoes was thrown at our hut. But Luke's father was not one of them, one of the few. He was used to come round at times, alway bringing some cakes, some vegetables from the garden, some milk or some eggs from his chickens."

"What did you talk about when they came round?"

"Well, when Luke's father came he would want to know what I had got up to in the war." replied Alina's father. "So I told him about myself and thousands of other Polish peoples who fought alongside the Allies in Italy to defeat the Nazis, and how I was one of the lucky ones to survive. He used to listen to me going on about how terrible it was, how awful it was to see your comrades shot dead beside you, how hard the conditions were in the Italian winter in the Apennine mountains, the many miles we had to march until we arrived in Rome. It was all as if it was something he would have liked to have been part of, something he missed out on. He is such a quiet man, a listener not a talker. Local folks don't seem to want to have much to do with him, for whatever reason. There was even talk that he may have played a part in the death of a pilot who was killed on the airfield, but that just seemed like idle gossip to us."

"Do you believe he had something to do with the pilot's death?"

"Not really" said her father, but her mother quickly interjected "Not at all. It's just the lies, the fake stuff people want to put around for their own reasons. I may not know what those reasons are but they would have reasons for making up something terrible like that. What are they saying, that he's a murderer or something? It's crazy. People tell lies just to try to get their own ideas out there, for their own selfish ends."

"Maybe they're not so much telling lies but hinting and suggesting that Luke's father may be guilty in some way or other" said Alina.

"In much ways that's worse still. It's like planting a seed in the back of their minds that they hope will grow. It's disgusting."

The next day Luke came round to Alina's home, and she came straight out before he could say hello to her parents.

"Let's go down to where that oak tree came down on the common." said Alina purposefully.

When they arrived they sat on top of the trunk of the oak, their feet well off the ground.

"I think it's about time to go over what we have found out about your pilot." said Alina.

"OK" replied Luke.

"We went to see the Flight Commander and he told us who the pilot was by looking at the pen you found, and how he had died. We went to see Mr Westwood and he told us what sort of person he was, how he liked to enjoy walking around the common. We went to see Mr and Mrs Hughes and they told us a bit more about him and how the womenfolk liked him. So where does this leave us?"

"I've got the pen here in my pocket" Luke replied, showing the pen to Alina as he spoke, "as I carry it round with me all the time now. It's told us a few things, but it's like a lane with lots of twists and bends, when you think you go round one corner you will be able to see the way ahead, but all you see is the next corner. As soon as we get some sort of an answer to one question we get another question in front of us. And is everyone telling us the truth, or are they telling us lies, or are they just not telling us the more important bits, just hinting at things?"

Alina bit her lip, although Luke didn't notice. "What is it we are trying to find out?" she said softly.

"And where was he buried?" said Luke, continuing his train of thought, not listening to Alina. "They all say anyone killed on the airfield or on flights from the airfield were buried in war graves in the local churchyard. Let's go and see if we can find his grave."

Alina sensed that now was not the time to talk to Luke about what she had found out the day before, so off they went.

The church with its small tower that provided a nesting site for swifts was set on the outskirts of a nearby village. The graveyard was for the most part not properly cared for, with many headstones grey with age and covered in lichens, lying on their backs, or at least well off the vertical. Just the more recent burials had smart black headstones with some flowers in a vase at the base. Luke knew the graveyard as his mother was buried there, although he had never visited the grave, and he pointed it out to Alina. She asked why it was not kept as well as many of the others, and Luke shrugged his shoulders. As they were standing there the rector, an elderly man dressed in black wearing a dog collar and with grey hair neatly parted, approached them. He had seen them enter the churchyard as he was putting up notices in the porch, and he went up to them in his customary hearty and rather brisk manner, with the air of someone who had authority and was happy to let others know it.

"Good day young people" said the rector. "And what brings you to this sacred place on such a blessed day?"

"We want to find the grave of one of the pilots who was killed on the airfield in the war." replied Luke.

"Ah, well now, you may find that along the hedge on the far side" said the rector, pointing with his finger. "Over there. All the people who were killed in the war are buried there, each one with a white headstone provided by the government. Our helpers try to make sure they are kept clean, so you should be able to find the name you are looking for."

Luke and Alina went over to the hedge and found a row of plain white headstones, all identical apart from the name and rank inscribed on them. After walking along the row, they stopped when they found the right one. There was a small posy of flowers at the foot of the headstone, all somewhat faded, but it was the only one of those graves with flowers.

"Flight Lieutenant James Craig. Killed on 30th September 1944." read out Luke.

They both stood in front of the grave for a while. "So, what have we learned?" asked Alina.

"At least we know that he had a proper burial. And that someone continues to visit his grave, unlike the rest of the graves. Someone still cares."

As they wandered away the rector called them over.

"Did you find what you were looking for?" he asked.

"Yes we did." replied Luke.

"Does anyone come and visit the war graves?" asked Alina.

"I hardly ever see anybody." replied the rector. "Where are you from?"

"Poland" said Alina.

"No, I didn't mean that, I meant .... where do you live?"

"I live by the common, and Alina lives in the camp nearby." said Luke.

"Are you one of the commoners' lads? asked the rector.

"Yes I look after some cattle on the common."

"So you'll be the son of that chap who keeps himself to himself then. Now that's a thankless task, just looking after a few cattle. Can't imagine that you would want to do that for ever for sure."

"I don't mind it most of the time, it's what I want to do, and I love the common." responded Luke, who was not being totally truthful as tending the cattle in all weathers was not his fondest pastime. But he was feeling that the rector was trying to influence him in some way.

At that moment a large car pulled up and a man wound down the window and shouted across at the rector.

"Still OK for the meeting tomorrow evening at the parish hall, rector?"

"Yes that's fine." replied the rector. "Six o'clock it is. Do the others know?"

"They know", and with that the car sped off.

"Do you know Sir Geoffrey?" said the rector looking at Luke. "Fine man, takes a great interest in what goes on around here. Always looking how things can be improved, which is what we all want, don't we."

Luke looked at Alina, puzzled. "What was that about?" he said looking at Alina, but the rector responded.

"Nothing you need to worry yourself about. Now, you need to be worrying yourself more about that father of yours. People round here know that he keeps himself to himself for a reason. No smoke without fire."

"What do you mean?" said Luke, raising his voice. "Why can't people tell me the honest truth about what happened and be straight with me. All I get to hear are hints and people giving me knowing looks."

"You'd be better off speaking to your father, and asking him for some answers. Now on your way, the pair of you."

"Come on" said Alina, and they got back onto their bicycles and went back towards the Polish camp. They stopped by the food van that came to the camp twice a week, each using their pocket money to buy choc ices, and sat down on the pavement to enjoy them.

"I try talking to my Dad but he just walks away, he doesn't want to talk to me about what happened in the past" said Luke.

"You're just going to have to try harder, make it more difficult for him to ignore you. Make it clear you won't accept him stonewalling you all the time. Even threaten to run away if he won't tell you what you need to know."

"Run away? Where to?"

"I don't know. Just make a threat. That could make him open up a bit."

"Not too sure about that, but you may be right."

"Luke, there's something I need to tell you. It may be hard for you, but you need to know. I went back to see the Flight Commander yesterday."

"Why did you do that?"

"Because I felt he wasn't telling us the full truth. And you know that the truth sometimes hurts."

"Go on."

"He told me that it was an open secret round about that your Dad was involved in checking the pilot's plane before the crash."

"So what? Are you saying that he was in some way responsible for the pilot's death?"

"When we went to see Bill Westwood he told us that the pilot was well liked by the women round here. And when we went to see Mr and Mrs Hughes they hinted that your mother and the pilot were....well...lovers. Can you not see what is being implied, what some people are saying?"

Luke was silent for a moment, before speaking very quietly and slowly.

"So you think that my Dad killed the pilot because he was jealous as the pilot and my Mum were lovers. And that's what everyone around here thinks. But nobody has told me."

"Luke, I don't think that, and my parents don't think that, but some other people think that. None of it may be right. Maybe your Dad had nothing to do with the pilot's death, maybe your Mum and the pilot weren't lovers. What do I know? Nothing really. But I think you need to find out a bit more. At the moment people are clearly going round saying and thinking these things, but you need to find out the truth. If you don't... well, these things will just stay and haunt you. And you need to find out why people are saying or hinting about these things, and what is true and what isn't."

"So what was all that about a meeting that the chap in the car shouted at the rector?" asked Luke, changing the subject.

"Search me" said Alina. "But there's only one way to find out."

"What's that?"

"Spy on them. There are things we are not being told. The only way to find out is to see if we can listen to what's being said at the meeting tomorrow evening."

"How are we going to do that?"

"Listen at the window."

"We can't do that. What if we get caught? No way. I'm off" and he got back on his bicycle and sped off across the common back home.

When he arrived home his father was cleaning out the chickens. Luke propped his bicycle against the back wall of the house and offered to make his father a mug of tea.

"That would be grand" his father said, "and I'll come inside to have it once I've finished here. Two eggs today, so egg and potatoes tonight."

Luke made the tea, stirring in just one spoonful of sugar straight out of the packet to both his and his father's mugs. He felt now was as good a time as any to confront his father with what people were saying about him despite the fact that there was little chance of getting anything out of him, but he had to try. He thought about Alina's idea of threatening to run away, but saw that as a last resort. So as soon as his father had washed his hands and sat down at the kitchen table he began, quietly and hesitatingly.

"You know the pilot who was killed on the airfield. Well, I've been speaking to people about him, and ..."

"You have, have you. I hope you don't believe everything they say" interrupted his father.

"Well, I'm just going to tell you what they have said, because I don't know what's true and what's not, and why they're saying any of it anyway. We, that's Alina the Polish girl and me."

"You mean your girlfriend" interrupted his father

"Please don't interrupt. Alina and I went to see the Flight Commander who lives nearby, and he talked to us about the plane crash. He said that one of the engines had caught fire and that the pilot could not escape in time because he couldn't open the window of the cockpit as it was jammed. And he told Alina that you had been responsible for checking the plane before it took off, and making sure everything was all right."

"He did, did he?"

"And then we went to see Mr and Mrs Hughes and they said that the pilot knew my mum, and that they were close friends. And Alina thinks that they meant that....you know.... they were more than just friends."

"She thinks that, does she?"

"And that, if you put the two things together, it makes out that, well, it seems like that you had it in for the pilot, to put it plainly."

There was a silence. Luke's father stood up, took the mug of tea in both of his hands and squeezed it so tightly that Luke thought it would shatter. He sat down again, put the mug down on the table, put his head in his hands and started sobbing. Luke remained silent. He had never seen his father like this before. The sobbing went on for what seemed to him like an eternity, but it was only a couple of minutes. Luke went over to his father and put his arm on his father's shoulder.

"Dad, you must tell me the truth. I need to know."

His father wiped his eyes and cleared his throat. "I'm sorry. You mother was the finest woman in the world, and I was the luckiest man in the world to have married her. There was nothing she wouldn't do for other people. At the funeral people told me what a wonderful teacher she was with the small children, and that the whole school had been terribly upset. She was kindness itself, it was all so natural to her, and such a good mother to you. Not a day goes by when I don't think of her."

"But Dad, tell me about the pilot and his plane."

"In the war I did help out looking after the planes, as I had some knowledge of mechanics and trained as ground crew. And I did work on that pilot's plane before it took off that evening. It was just another training flight, practising flying at night. You've got to know that the planes they were flying were pretty clapped out. They had already flown hundreds of missions over Germany, but they were all we had. I know that in the enquiry into the crash they found that the pilot's window mechanism was faulty, but so were many things with the planes. They said that the reason the pilot caught fire and died was that he couldn't get out in time. He was an experienced and highly regarded pilot, and he did brilliantly to make sure the crew got out in time and to land the plane as he did amongst the heather rather than the buildings where the crews were stationed. The window was not something I had looked at or was aware of as a problem. I had to give evidence to the enquiry, but in their conclusions they didn't point the finger at me, but some people did. One of the engines had caught fire, and that was nothing to do with me, it was just an accident waiting to happen with an old aircraft."

"So why did some people point the finger at you? Was it about my mother and the pilot?"

"I can't tell you."

"Why not?"

Luke's father took out a handkerchief and wiped his eyes and blew his nose.

"You may not like what I say, and I don't want to see you being hurt."

"Look Dad, I'm old enough now, I'm not a young child anymore. I need to have the truth. Too many people are hinting and gossiping about things which I don't know about. That hurts. Not knowing the truth hurts more than knowing a painful truth."

A long pause.

"Is there more tea in the pot, son?"

Luke got up and poured his father another mug of tea, with another one spoonful of sugar.

"Every time I look at you I see her. And I don't want to hurt you as I would be hurting her. She still lives with me, if you can understand that."

"I can, Dad, I can."

"It's difficult for me." Another long pause. "You know your auntie Jean at Orchard Farm, your mother's sister? She knows what happened. She would be able to explain it all better than I can. I'll ask her to call round here, and you can ask her all your questions. She's a sensible woman, and can give you the answers you're looking for."

"Thanks Dad. And I do understand, I really do."

"And as for all the gossip, much of it is about us commoners. You see, we're not liked much around here, people see us as clinging onto the past, as a relic from a bygone age, and that's all part of it. Now the war's long over they think it's a new world, one where the likes of us don't belong. They try and make life uncomfortable for us, us and the Poles. Your auntie Jean, although she and her husband haven't got the commoners' rights like us, she understands all that too."

Luke left his father and went upstairs and lay on his bed. He took the pen and held it between his fingers, twisting it round and round, thinking about the man who had held it and what stories the pen might yet be able to tell.

That evening Alina left her home, quietly slipping out unbeknown to her parents when they were busy outside in their small garden, and running most of the way to the parish hall. It was another of the former wartime buildings, a wooden hut amongst a stand of pine trees, near to the church. There were three cars parked outside, including Sir Geoffrey's. She worked out that the best way to hear what was being said was to get as close as possible to the windows. She could hear voices but making out the words was difficult. She needed to be higher up, and she spotted a steel crate used for milk bottles nearby. Carrying this over, she stood on it on tiptoe so that her eyes could just see into the room, and when she pressed her ear against the window she could make out some of the words being spoken.

She could see Sir Geoffrey, the rector and Mr and Mrs Hughes, whom she and Luke had met a couple of days ago. They were all gathered round a table with some papers in the middle, including what looked like a map, maybe the same map she and Luke had seen at the Hughes' farmhouse. As Alina stood on tiptoe so the milk crate tipped this way and that. Sir Geoffrey was speaking. "Don't worry, don't worry about any of that, I'll make sure there's no problems there."

"What about that commoner with his cattle?" said another voice.

"Him?" said someone else, with a snigger followed by a laugh.

Alina became unsteady, and she felt the crate tip over as she fell off, landing on the ground. She sensed that the noise would disturb the people inside, so she ran round the back and into the pine trees. Sure enough, she heard the door of the hall open and then a voice, she thought probably belonging to the rector, shouted "Who's there?" Alina kept completely still, trying not even to breathe, feeling the chill of the early autumn air on her face. She then heard footsteps and the door of the hall close. She felt it was all right to move again, and she started to make her way back home. She thought about what was being talked about at the meeting. Why was it all so secretive? Why were just those people there? Perhaps they were talking about putting up a memorial to the pilot who was killed, but then why wasn't the Flight Commander present? Perhaps it was really nothing to do with her and Luke anyway, and they were just being curious nosey-parkers after all.

But then she heard footsteps behind her, running footsteps. She turned round and saw the figure of a man, froze for a moment, and then ran. She ran as quickly as she could, her heart beating rapidly and her breath getting shorter and shorter. The night was pitch black, and in the darkness she found it difficult to pick her way through the pine trees without getting caught and tripped by the brambles. Although she ran as quickly as she could the man soon caught up with her and he grabbed her by the arm.

"So what's a pretty young girl like you doing out in the woods at night?"

Alina struggled, but the man's large hand had a firm grip right around her arm. She tried to punch the man, but he succeeded in grabbing hold of her other arm and pulling her closer to him. As she looked into his face she recognised that it belonged to Mr Hughes.

Mr Hughes looked straight into Alina's eyes, and spoke slowly and deliberately in a voice full of rage. "You think you can spy on us, do you, young girl? Do you think that you and that boyfriend of yours can start interfering? Well let me teach you a lesson you're not going to forget in any sort of hurry."

He threw Alina to the ground.

"No, please no"

He then picked her up with one arm and walked her so that she was stepping backwards until her back met a tree trunk. He put his left arm against her shoulder pressing her body against the tree and with his other hand he gently lifted her dress and stroked her upper thigh, moving his other hand to hold her by the throat.

"Now then, what exactly is a pretty young girl like you doing running in the woods at night? I'll tell you what she's doing. She's being very, very naughty. I've already told her not to go round poking her Polish nose into other people's business, haven't I?" He continued to rub his hand up and down Alina's thigh, whilst Alina stood completely still, eyes looking at the ground as she couldn't bring herself to look him in the face. "And if I hear that she has been naughty again, well now, I could make her life very uncomfortable indeed, and it might be something she would never be able to forget …"

Rather than talk, he began to whisper into Alina's ear.

"..I'm sure you wouldn't want that to happen, would you? All you have to do is behave yourself and you'll be all right. But if you don't behave yourself, it will all be your own fault."

Alina summoned as much strength as she could and pushed him away. She pulled down her dress and spat at Mr Hughes, hitting him in the face, before turning round and running off. Before she had gone very far, and after looking round to check that she wasn't being followed, she sat down and started to shake as the tears flowed. When she had wiped away her tears she walked slowly home.

Her mother asked her where she has been and commented on the state of her dress, but Alina ignored her. Her father, however, had something else to say to her as she tried to make her way towards her bedroom.

"You can stay here. There's something we need to say to you."

Alina swung round, stopped and pulled up a chair by the kitchen table.

"OK, what is it?"

"Your mother and I want you to return to Poland. It is time you learnt more about your heritage and culture, and just staying here means you are going to become totally like an English person."

"But we've already been over this, and I don't want to go. I like it here, this is my home now."

"We've made our decision, we've booked the tickets and off you will go. Your aunts and uncles can't wait to set eyes on you again, to see what a wonderful niece they have, and you will be able to meet your cousins. And you can learn more about Poland, the country where you were born."

"But....but....I belong here, by the common." Alina replied unconvincingly, as she knew deep down it was a hopeless fight, and that she might as well give in. Her head bowed, she walked slowly out of the kitchen and into her bedroom.

The next day as Luke was tending his cattle on the common Alina arrived.

"Can we talk?" she said in an uncharacteristically subdued and hesitant voice.

"Are you feeling OK?" replied Luke, bending his head to look into her eyes as she held her head down.

"Not really. The thing is I can't talk to my Mum and Dad, and you're really the only friend I've got. It's about what happened last night."

"You mean you actually went round to the parish hall and tried to spy on the meeting? Alina, that was a pretty stupid thing to do."

"It's not just that, and please don't be cross with me."

She wiped away tears from her eyes and she sat down on the grass, and Luke sat next to her.

"They heard me, and that Mr Hughes followed me as I ran off, and he tried to put his hand up my dress, threatening to, well you know..."

Luke was stunned, and for a while he could not find the right words to say.

"That's dreadful. You poor girl." He moved to put his arm around her shoulder, but she flinched.

"Please don't touch me" and then after a pause "I hate him. I spat at him."

Luke felt out if his depth, not knowing whether to say words of comfort, which could sound trite or hollow, or something to reflect the hurt and anger Alina was obviously feeling.

"I've got to make him pay" continued Alina, as she found her normal, stronger voice. "He's not going to be able to get away with this, never."

"What do you mean?" asked Luke.

"I'll think of something. He's got to pay for this."

"You can't be serious. You're not going to try another stunt are you, putting yourself in danger again."

"Luke, it may not be your way, but it's my way. I know you like talking more, trying to talk to people, understand them more, but that's not really me. I prefer doing something to make my point."

"Yes, but you might well make matters worse that way. Sometimes you should be more patient, less headstrong. I feel that there is a lot going on round here that we don't fully understand. Why did Mr Hughes react in that way? Was he worried that you may have found something out? Why were he and his wife making pointed comments about my mother? We need to find out more, ask more questions, ask the right questions."

"Well you can carry on with your questions, but not me. I don't care so much about why he did what he did, more that he did it, and that he's going to pay for it. Luke, you've been a real help."

"Don't feel I've done much."

"Yes you have, you've listened, and that's really important."

Alina got to her feet, and she gave Luke a kiss on the cheek.

"Take care" said Luke as she walked away.

4.

An Unwelcome Intruder

Luke had known his auntie Jean all his life as she was his mother's sister. She was a social worker in the children's department of the local council, and was experienced in helping children in trouble, sometimes removing them from their parents with legal authority and into foster care if they were being ill-treated. She had a natural understanding and kindness that she had shared with her younger sister, Luke's mother. But she also possessed more of a grounded and sensible nature, in contrast to her sister whom she saw as more head-in-the-clouds. In the years after Luke's mother had died she had spent a lot of time with Luke and his father, often inviting them round to her house for meals where they could discuss farming matters as she and her husband had a smallholding with a few sheep and cattle.. She understood how the death of his mother had affected Luke, and had tried to give him the time and space to put his feelings into words as she knew this was something his father could not do.

She called round the next evening as Luke's father had asked her to. When she arrived Luke's father left the house saying he would be going for a walk on the common, but not before he told Luke to make her a cup of tea. When the tea was made they both sat down at the kitchen table.

"Luke, your father has told me that you have been asking him questions about you mother. Tell me what are the questions that you need answers to?"

"People are saying that my Mum and the pilot who was killed on the airfield got to know each other well, and they seem to be saying that they were…well…."

"Lovers who slept together?"

"Well, yes, sort of, although they weren't saying that in so many words."

"No, but it is what they meant. How does that make you feel?"

"Sort of upset really. More than that….angry, I suppose."

"Angry with them, angry with who?"

"The people who were saying these things. Or rather hinting at them. Mr and Mrs Hughes to start with. And the rector. I just need to know the truth."

"Luke, are you angry with your mother, or your father?"

"I don't know if it's true or not, if they were, like you say, lovers."

"You may say that the only two people who would be able to give you an honest answer, your Mum and the pilot, are both dead now. What has your father said to you about this?"

"Nothing. Except to invite you round as he thinks you would be able to give me some honest answers."

"Perhaps nobody else knows for certain what happened, apart from those two people. So let's assume that they were in fact lovers. What difference would that make to you?"

"My mum was the best mum in the world." Luke's eyes filled with tears. "And I don't want people going round saying she was a bad person, that she did something to be ashamed of, that she did something very wrong."

Jean took a deep breath. "Luke, your mother and I were sisters, and that is why your father asked me to come round and speak with you. We spent many hours at my house talking about many things. She told me how proud she was of you, how she loved you and how she enjoyed watching you grow up."

Luke could not help but smile despite the fact that he was wiping away tears as he heard those words.

"And she also told me about the pilot."

"What did she tell you about the pilot?"

Jean's voice softened. "Luke, when you love someone you want to tell the whole world about it. It makes you feel that full of emotion, so joyful and so happy. Sometimes it just happens that two people meet and fall in love, no matter what their circumstances are, it just happens. Your mother told me about it, how handsome he was, how kind he was, how gentle he was towards her, how she loved to hear his voice and look into his eyes, how he made her smile for no obvious reason. Sometimes reason does not play a part in love. They tried to keep it a secret, meeting where and when they could, often on the common, but round here that's almost impossible. They were lovers, of course they were, and it is nothing for you or anyone else to be critical of, or to be embarrassed about or angry or ashamed of. Your mum wouldn't want you to feel that way. To her it was one of the most amazing and beautiful times of her life, and it all happened towards the end of her life, even though she didn't realise that at the time, and in fact towards the end of both of their lives."

She moved closer to Luke and took his hand in hers.

"You know that she died very suddenly from an infection, and a few weeks later the pilot was killed on the common. She told me she tore her dress and sustained a bad cut to her leg from trying to climb over the barbed wire on the airfield perimeter fence when going to meet the pilot one day after school. Two lives, young lives, both gone before their time. Both too young to die. Some would say that they are together now, but that's not how I see it, as we all have just one life. That was their time, and I am sure neither of them would want their lives to be any different if they could have their time over again. To them being together was so beautiful."

Luke drank from his mug of tea, swallowing hard. Although he listened to what his aunt was saying, he found it difficult to take it all in, let alone understand it all. He recalled seeing a

49

fragment of material on the barbed wire fence the night of the plane crash. There was a long silence.

"I can hardly remember her funeral, I was just in a daze."

"It was a very difficult time for everybody. Your father couldn't cope with any of it – the fact that his wife had found someone else, her dying, trying to help you – I don't think he has ever grieved properly. He probably feels he lost her twice – once to the pilot, and once to death – and has never come to terms with either of these.

"So why are people making these comments, making me feel as though I had a bad mother, which is just so untrue? And why are they saying that my father had a part to play in the pilot's death?"

"Luke, do you seriously believe your father would ever intentionally cause anyone's death? Do you really believe that? He has spoken to me when he invited me round here to talk to you. He told me what he told you about him checking the pilot's plane. It's clear he was telling the truth, as he told it to the enquiry. You may say that your dad is an odd sort in some way, keeping himself to himself and not being good at showing his feelings, and that's how a lot of people round here were brought up, but he was never a liar. He would never tell deliberate falsehoods, just as he was never a murderer. It's not in his nature."

"So why are people saying these things?"

"Your dad is a commoner, he has the commoner's rights, and the two of you are the only ones left putting out their animals to graze the common. Now, at this time, the talk is all of progress, and the commoners and their rights are just seen as an obstacle to progress, whatever that is. It's as though you're in the way, you're something to get rid of. Years ago the commoners were respected as guardians of tradition, of a way of looking after the land, but not anymore. We have a small farm here, as you know, and me and my husband look after our land in a traditional way, a conventional way of farming that has been passed down through generations, with respect to our animals and to the land that provides for us. We don't have the commoner's rights like your dad, but we admire him, and you for that matter for keeping a tradition alive. And we've always supported the commoners, especially your dad and people like Bill Westwood. People these days see the common itself as a bit of an anomaly, something obsolete, something not in tune with the modern ways. It's something you're going to have to get used to, the constant snide comments, making out you're little more than a nuisance, a barrier to so-called economic progress. Don't let it get you down, don't let them win, don't ever give in."

"Thanks" said Luke. "It helps, it helps a lot.

"But do you understand why people are trying to put you down?"

"I think I do, but it's all a lot to take in" replied Luke. "And thanks for coming round" he continued as his aunt stood up and made her way out. Luke went slowly upstairs, went into his room and found the fountain pen. He twisted it in his fingers, wondering how many more truths it would lead him towards. He wondered if his mother had ever seen the pen when she was with the pilot. Perhaps she had seen him write with it. The pen had now brought him closer to his mother, as well to the pilot, her lover. Where else would it take him?

A few days later Luke got up early as usual to check on his cattle. He moved them from one part of the common to another where he knew there was better grazing available for them. He had his favourites, especially one called Florence, who was more timid than the rest.

"Come on Florence, move it." he said tapping her with a stick as she had become detached from the rest of the group, preferring to eat some grass before catching up with the rest.

As he walked the cattle across the common he heard voices near the roadside, and he saw a tractor with a group of men around it. Thinking nothing of it, he carried on moving the cattle. But Florence became detached again, looking round. She had seen the group of men and it had clearly made her anxious, lowing loudly. Luke had to go back and get her again, but he also looked round and could see that the tractor had moved onto the common, and that there was a second tractor behind it. Once he had arrived with the cattle at the better grazing he decide he'd better go and investigate, so he left the cattle and walked back across the common to where the tractors were. As he got close the first of the tractors started to move, and it was closely followed by the second, and then a third towing a trailer came into view. He stopped in puzzlement as to what was going on. He was still some distance from the men, some of whom had now climbed aboard the tractors to drive them. He decided to watch from a distance rather than get too close.

The first tractor towed a mower which started to cut the heather and the grasses. Once this was a little way ahead the other two tractors followed behind. The first of these towed a machine that went over the cuttings and blew them up into a chute, and they went into the big trailer being towed by the third tractor which drove alongside. The common was being mown again, as it had been when the airfield was built. Luke saw skylarks fly up and away as the tractors drove on, and a hare run for cover, as well as the rabbits.

Luke sat down, wondering why on earth the common was being mown again. He thought that maybe he should go up to the men and ask them, or maybe he should go home and ask his dad if he knew. Where was Alina? He wanted her there, and without her he did not feel confident enough to go up to the men and ask them why they were mowing the common again. He felt that his cattle would be all right where they were, some distance from the tractors, and went home.

His dad was sitting at the breakfast table when he arrived.

"Cattle OK?" he asked when Luke came through the door. "There's some tea left in the pot. Help yourself to some toast."

Luke didn't answer his father's question or take up the offer of a cup of tea.

"Why are they mowing the common?"

"What?" replied Luke's father.

"Why are they mowing the common dad? I've just seen three tractors on there, cutting all the heather and everything and collecting all that they've cut and blowing it into a trailer. Why are they doing it? It's just like when the airfield was here."

"You're joking."

"I've just been out there and seen it clear as day."

"Come on, let's go and see what's going on."

Luke's father hastily put down his mug of tea, got up, put his coat on and went outside, with Luke following close behind. They walked quickly to where the tractors were and two people were stood watching the mowing.

Luke recognised Mr and Mrs Hughes from Orchard Farm. Luke's father walked up to them and started speaking.

"Right, what's afoot here?"

"Nowt to do with you."

"Everything to do with me. I've got commoners' rights on this land."

"Means nothing."

"What?" shouted Luke's father.

"Don't lose your rag, dad." said Luke, trying to calm him.

"Lose my rag? What on earth do you think you are doing? This is the common. They're not allowed on here. Tell your guys to get those machines off here right now."

"No chance." replied Mr Hughes, who then walked away a short distance with his wife, leaving Luke and his father standing alone together in stunned silence.

"We've got to do something." said Luke after a while.

"They're criminals." said his father, beginning to regain his composure. "I don't know what to do, but we've got to do something. What's the point of all this mowing? Why are they doing it?"

"We've got commoners rights to have our grazing animals on here, and you are destroying the grazing. You have no right to do this" Luke's father shouted at Mr Hughes.

Mr Hughes turned away. The tractor drivers wheeled round at the end of their pass, stopped briefly before Mr Hughes told them to carry on and they proceeded to mow more of the heather and grasses. As they disappeared into the distance two skylarks flew up, as well as a host of butterflies and moths.

"What are we going to do?" Luke asked his father. "Can we phone the police?"

"I don't know if they could do anything. We're going to go home and make some phone calls to see if we can find out what is going on."

They walked home, with Luke running to keep up with his father's speedy walk. At home Luke's father phoned various people he knew around the common but none of them knew why the common was being mown again.

"I'm going back out there" said Luke, hastily running out of the door and he was soon on the common again. The mown heather had been piled up and was now a big bonfire. But now he noticed there was a change. Instead of two tractors running, one mowing and the other being driven alongside collecting the heather and grass cuttings in a trailer, there was now just one. As he got nearer he could see that the one tractor that was working was no longer mowing. Closer still, he saw that it was ploughing. What was left of the heather and the grasses were being ripped out and turned over, exposing the bare, sandy soil. He ran up to Mr Hughes who continued to supervise the work. But Luke was speechless. He did not know how to express his feelings at seeing the common being destroyed in front of his eyes. It was as if he was witnessing a rape, or even a killing. He felt traumatised by the violence. Something he had cherished throughout his life was being violated and wrecked in just one morning.

The tractor driving the plough was approaching them when Luke saw a familiar figure approaching. It was the butterfly woman, running as fast as she could, butterfly net in hand. She marched up to Mr Hughes.

"You stop that infernal machine immediately." she told him, but he just turned away. She hit Mr Hughes across the legs with the wooden handle of her net.

"You evil, evil man. Don't you realise what you are destroying?" Mr Hughes did not respond.

The tractor drew nearer and the plough was raised as it turned round to begin another pass. As it started to plough again the butterfly woman overtook the plough and lay down on the mown heather directly in front of the tractor. The tractor stopped. It reversed, and then started moving forward again just to the side of the woman, but she got up and lay down in front of it again.

At this point a police constable arrived on the scene, getting off his bicycle and laying it carefully on the ground. Luke guessed that it must have been his father who had phoned the police. The policeman walked up to stand beside the tractor, with the butterfly woman still lying on the ground in front of it.

"I've been asked to attend because someone phoned the station and said there is some damage being done to the common." he said, in an officious tone.

"Too bloody right there is" said the butterfly woman.

"And your name is...." said the constable.

"Crumble" she replied.

"Now Mrs Crumble...."

"Miss, if you don't mind".

"I beg your pardon" said the constable. "Can you please tell me, Miss Crumble, why you are lying in front of the tractor?"

"I take it that the reason you have been asked to come here is because of these vandals" she replied, pointing her butterfly net at Mr Hughes and the tractor drivers.

"Well, Miss, that may be the case, but..."

Mr Hughes interrupted him. "This woman is preventing our men from doing what is perfectly within the law. This land is needed to grow crops to provide British food for British people. We intend to use the land to grow potatoes, and to do that we need to get rid of the heather and turn over the soil."

"I am aware that this is the common, so by what right can you do this?" asked the constable.

"By the say-so of the owner. We are doing this through his agent, and you can ring him up and check it if you like."

The constable paused. Meanwhile Miss Crumble got to her feet and approached the constable.

"Don't you understand?" She put her hand in her pocket and pulled out a small glass pot with a cardboard lid. Inside the pot was a small blue butterfly, fluttering. She stared the constable in the face, almost nose to nose. "This butterfly is rare. This butterfly is rare because this", at which point she spread her right arm out wide and gestured at the heather on the common "is rare. All the rest of the heath in this part of the world has been destroyed by the plough or by having houses built on it or trees planted on it, and this is the only bit left, and these, these vandals, these greedy, greedy vandals want to plough this up to make money. And then the butterfly and all the other wildlife will be gone completely. They just see an opportunity to grow some potatoes so that they can make money. And it should be your job to stop them"

"Now Miss Crumble" said the constable, in the placid tone he had become use to adopting whenever he came across what he saw as a minor disturbance, "I don't know anything about your butterfly. But these people tell me they are acting within the law and I have no reason to doubt them. So I would be very grateful if you would make sure you don't cause a breach of the peace and let these gentlemen continue with their lawful business. And in the meantime, if you wish, I suggest you contact your solicitor if you think you have a case against them. Gentlemen" he said turning to Mr Hughes and the tractor driver, "Carry on with your work."

"You" shouted Miss Crumble at Luke, marching over towards him and pushing the wooden handle of her butterfly net into his stomach. "You look after your cattle here on the common. Why aren't you doing something about this, this destruction. The common is your birthright, your heritage, defend it for heaven's sake."

Luke looked at her, and looked at the constable. "She's right. Please stop them from ploughing up the common."

Miss Crumble sighed and stared at Luke. "Pathetic" was all she said.

"I'll be getting on then. Good day to you all, and I don't want to hear of any more nonsense."

With that he got back on his bicycle and rode off the common. The tractor driver climbed back onto the tractor, started the engine, lowered the plough and began ploughing another furrow.

Miss Crumble walked up to Mr Hughes. "You haven't heard the last from me" she said, and swiftly walked away. Luke was left rooted to the spot. He had forgotten about his father, and there was only one person he knew he needed to see. He ran in the direction of Alina's house, shouting her name as he ran. When he arrived there he knocked at the front door but there was no answer. He went to the back of the house, shouting her name, when he saw Alina's parents in the garden tending their vegetable patch.

"Where's Alina?"

"She left this morning" replied her father.

"Left? Where she's gone?"

"She's gone to Poland to spend time with members of her family there. She'll be away for a while."

Luke stood completely still. He could feel tears starting to from in his eyes, so he turned away immediately, muttered a quick thank you and walked slowly home, not being up to return to the common and witness what was happening there, wiping his eyes as he went.

Over the next few days the mowing and the ploughing continued until over half of the common had been lost to cultivation, but not all of it. Then the harrow came on to break up the soil, followed by hundreds of tons of chicken manure from local chicken farms, which was then turned into the soil. The stench was horrendous.

Luke could still find space for his cattle, but it saddened his heart each time he went onto the common. The farm workers told him to keep off the cultivated areas, land he had known all his life as his playground, his home for his cattle, his own place that more than anything else defined who he was. He was the young lad on the common, and now the common was being killed off in front of his eyes. All the creatures that he had become so familiar with, the birds, the butterflies, the rabbits, the stoats and foxes, whilst not completely absent, had been driven out into what little remained of the heath on the common.

Luke felt so powerless, and he looked to his father for an idea, any idea, about what they could do to stop all of this. But his father was bereft of ideas, and all he could say was that it was people with money who ruled the world and decided what was going to happen. Rich men could do what they liked and there wasn't any law to stop them. He said he could plead with them as much as he could but it would all be wasted breath.

Luke stayed with his cattle on what was left of the common. Sometimes the cattle would walk over to the bare soil where the crops would soon be growing and gaze at it. Luke thought they knew that it was their land by rights, that it was their territory where they should be able to graze.

Sometimes he thought about Alina, and what she had been saying to him about his father, about the pilot, about his mother. He felt a sense of guilt that maybe he had been thinking about all those things and lost sight of the danger facing the common itself. All the things that Alina and others had been suggesting, that maybe his mother had had an affair, that maybe his father had been responsible for the death of the pilot, seemed strangely inconsequential now. His auntie Jean had helped him with these concerns anyway, and now he had to deal with some harsh realities in the present rather than think about the past.

Sometimes people would walk up to him, local people used to walking their dogs on the common, and share a sense of disbelief over what had been allowed to happen, but not offering any sort of remedy. He tried to think of what he could do, or might do, or should do, to but nothing came to him. Until one of the dog walkers suggested that what he should do was arrange a public meeting, to get everyone who was interested in the common together in the parish hall one evening and see if a plan would emerge. The man even offered to pay for the hire of the hall.

Luke walked back home, but before he went inside he saw two cars parked on the track by his house. He entered the house and found two men sitting with his father round the kitchen table. The two men looked up at Luke, and he recognised one of them. It was Mr Hughes.

"Well, there's something to think on. Let me know in a few days what you decide" said Mr Hughes to Luke's father as he got up and went towards the door.

59

"You know where I am, just call round" he said as both men left.

Luke looked at his father, who still had his head bowed.

"I know one of the men was Mr Hughes, but who was the other one, the one wearing the smart suit?" asked Luke.

"A chap who called himself Mr Biggar. Said he was something to do with the common."

"What did they want?"

"They wanted to give me money."

"What? Why would they want to do that? We're not that poor."

"They want to buy our commoners rights off me."

"What! They can't do that, surely."

"They're prepared to give me money, give us money, and it would come in useful."

Luke took his time before speaking again, trying to digest what his father had just said.

"They can't do that, can they?"

"They say it's all perfectly above board. Offered me £200. Told them I'd think about it."

"If you give them your rights then there would be nobody grazing the common, and they would no doubt plough all of it."

"We could do with the money though. Could do a lot here with the £200. Tidy up the yard, keep the house a bit warmer in the winters. And I'm getting no younger as far as looking after these cattle is concerned, and you may well want to move away in a few years' time. Could be an opportunity. Could be something we shouldn't pass up. Money talks in the real world"

"Dad, you should never surrender your rights to these people. It would spell the end of the common, not just for us but for everyone, and their children and their children. Once it's gone it's gone. We can't accept this."

"Any offer like that should be given proper consideration, that's all I'm saying."

"You...cannot...accept...it. It would be betraying what your father stood for, and all the commoners down the years have stood for."

His father shrugged his shoulders, and sighed. "Maybe... maybe. Leave it with me to sleep on."

Luke went on to tell his father that one of the dog walkers on the common had suggested holding a public meeting, but got no response save for another shrug of the shoulders. If he was to go ahead with the idea Luke knew that he would need help to set up a public meeting, and it disappointed him that his first choice of Alina was no longer around. He would have to approach the rector, for not only would he need his permission to use the parish hall but also he thought the rector would be able to tell people about the meeting, either through his weekly parish notices or through his personal contact with his parishioners.

When Luke called round to the church a few days later he found the rector sat on a bench outside with pen and paper in his hand. Luke went up to him and the rector looked up from his writing and said:

"Ah. The boy from the common. How can I help you?"

"Well, I was just wondering if I could use the parish hall for a meeting sometime soon."

"And what kind of a meeting might that be?"

"It would be a meeting about what's happening on the common."

"I see." The rector paused for a moment. "And what sort of a meeting about what's happening on the common?"

"It would be a public meeting so that everyone can come along."

"I see" said the rector, pausing again. "And what would the purpose be in that?"

"A lot of people are unhappy with the fact that much of the common has been ploughed up, and they don't agree with it. So it will give them an opportunity to express their views."

"But not everyone has a problem with the land being used more productively, to grow much needed food. Times have changed. Progress is coming to this sleepy backwater. And if you have a public meeting you will get all sides of an argument. Well I suppose you can have it for one evening. No violence mind, and no damage. You can make a booking with Mrs Bower, she lives in the bungalow just the other side of the church."

"Thanks rector" said Luke, happy that he had got permission, but nevertheless clearer in his own mind where the rector stood on the issue. As he walked away he thought back to the time when he and Alina had found the pilot's grave, and the rector had hinted then about changes that were planned and warnings that he and Alina had not heeded. The clues had been there, they had both seen Mr Hughes with a map of the common, but they had not understood, had not listened intensely enough to grasp what was about to happen. Luke had instead given his attention to the rumours and gossip about his parents. The pilot's pen had led them there, but they had not interpreted the meaning of the messages they had heard. Luke took the pen out of his pocket and looked at it as if it possessed some magic that would lead him in the right direction. He went round to Mrs Bower's bungalow and made a booking for the meeting in a fortnight's time.

The next thing he had to do was to publicise the meeting. Back at home he sat down at the kitchen table and talked to his father about what he might do, and they both decided that the best plan would be to display a poster around the area. Luke needed paper and writing materials, and it occurred to him that it would be an opportunity to use the pilot's pen. He went into the nearby town on his bicycle, walked into the newsagents and bought some foolscap paper, a set of crayons, a small jar of black ink, some drawing pins and sticky tape. Whilst he was there he showed the newsagent the pilot's pen and asked him if he could say anything about it. The newsagent held the pen gently, twisting it round in his fingers.

"It's a very fine pen, a Watermans, although clearly not in the best of condition. It would have cost a pretty price when new, and, if it was bought as a present, it would have been a mighty fine one, a lovely gift."

Back home in his bedroom he sat on his bed and took hold of the pen. He placed the jar of ink on his bedside table and removed the lid. Unscrewing the cap of the pen he placed the nib in the ink and with his finger pulled the metal lever on the side of the pen down so that it sucked up ink. He then wiped the pen on a piece of paper and holding it between his fingers started to write. He was surprised how well the pen wrote, how easy it was, and how it made him write better than his usual scrawl. He put the pen down and picked up one of the crayons, for clearly they would make the bigger letters that would be needed for the poster. He paused to think about what to write. After a while he wrote in red crayon in large capital letters: WHAT IS HAPPENING TO OUR COMMON? Then he picked up the pen and wrote also in large capital letters: PUBLIC MEETING ON 4th DECEMBER AT 7.30PM AT THE PARISH HALL – ALL WELCOME. He made twenty posters in all, which took him a whole evening.

Over the next few days Luke went around the common with a box of drawing pins and some sticky tape fixing the posters to trees, noticeboards, lamp posts, telephone boxes, bus stops, letter boxes, and benches. He cycled two miles into the nearest town and gave copies of the poster to various shops for them to display in their windows. He went into the office of the local weekly newspaper and gave them a copy to publicise in their next edition. He knocked on doors round about to tell people about the meeting. He nailed one to the front door of his house, and gave one to Alina's parents for them to display in a window. He felt energised that now, with the help of local people, something may be done to save the common.

On one occasion, as he was pinning a poster to a fence post next to a farm gate along a road which people used to walk into the town a man walked up across the field and shouted at him.

"What are you up to?"

"I'm just pinning a notice to the post here."

"Give it here." Luke unpinned the poster and handed it to the man, who read it.

"This is my land and my fence post. We don't need any public meetings round here, nor any posters. The public can get lost as far as I am concerned, and we don't need them interfering with us farmers." With that he tore up the poster into small pieces, gathered them together in his hand and stuffed them into the chest pocket of Luke's shirt. "Good day to you."

Luke, as ever, took it to heart, and wondered how many more of the posters would get torn down. He also remembered the words of his auntie Jean – don't let them get you down, don't let them win and don't ever give up. Other people he spoke to as he cycled round the area were more encouraging in their response, including one or two farmers who said that ploughing up the common was just giving farming a bad name. He was unsure, however, how many of them would come to the meeting, as maybe they would just give lip-service but, when it came to it, prefer to remain at home by the fire on a cold night.

He decided to visit Bill Westwood, who he knew would be supportive. When he called round Mr Westwood was leaving his house and locking the door.

"Young Luke, what's bothering you now."

"I was wondering if you would put this poster up in your window and come along to the meeting at the parish hall."

Mr Westwood took the poster, read it and pushed it through his letterbox.

"Champion. I'll be there. I'm just off to The Fox for some refreshment, so walk with me and tell me about what's going on."

Luke left his bicycle on the ground and walked alongside Mr Westwood, who walked with a stick and sometimes grabbed Luke with his other arm for more support. "Not as fit as a flea no more" he said.

"You know about the ploughing I suppose" began Luke.

"Know about it! I have been up there and given them all a piece of my mind. But how did it all happen? I for one knew nothing about it, and they kept it all as quiet as death. And death is the name of their game, as they're killing the common. You and your dad spend more time on the common than me, so didn't you have any inkling?"

"Not really, but looking back, in talking to some people, perhaps I should have sensed something was being planned. I got distracted by what people were saying to me, rather than picking up what they didn't want me to know. They laid false trails, and I stupidly believed them and followed them."

"There's a lesson there, the world is full of liars and people who will try to persuade you of all sorts of made-up nonsense, just for their own ends. So you have to question people's motives all the time. It's not just a case of what they may be saying, but why are the saying that, and why are they not talking about something else."

"I know, and that's a lesson I've now learnt."

"Well we'll see what comes of the public meeting then Luke, won't we. Any idea who's going to turn up?"

"None. It was a suggestion made by one of the people out on the common walking their dog, not my idea."

With that they had arrived outside The Fox. "See you at the meeting then Luke, and good night to you" said Mr Westwood as he stepped inside the pub.

The day of the meeting arrived. Luke was nervous, unable to keep still whether he was in his house or out on the common with the cattle. He walked up to the areas which had been ploughed up, and now felt a mixture of dismay at what had happened and hope that the meeting later on that day might herald something better. His hope was pinned on believing that the voice of the public could and should bring about a halt to the ploughing.

Luke and his father were the first to arrive at the parish hall, having first picked up the key from Mrs Bower. It was raining and it was cold, but that did not dampen Luke's sprits. All the chairs were stacked against the walls, so they spread them out in rows all facing the front. They then placed a table at the front with two chairs behind for themselves. People began to arrive, some of whom Luke recognised, his aunt Jean and the Flight Commander being two, and some not. They sat down, as near to the back as they could. More people arrived, including the rector and the police officer who had come onto the common the day the ploughing had started. The hall filled up, and Luke counted over fifty people. He was glad that so many people had come. He whispered to his father that he did not recognise some of the people, and his father replied that neither did he. It was time to start.

Luke's father stood up and began. "Good evening ladies and gentlemen." But people were still talking amongst themselves, so he banged on the table three times with his knuckles. The voices subsided.

"Good evening ladies and gentlemen, and welcome to this public meeting. I'm not really used to speaking in public at all, so you'll have to bear with me as I know I'm not really cut out for this kind of thing. I want to start by thanking you all for coming out despite the weather, and I trust this is a mark of how much we as local people care about the common. My son Luke sitting next to me here arranged this meeting so I would like to thank him. Many of you have probably seen him on the common looking after our cattle. In the last few weeks the land available for cattle grazing in accordance with our rights as commoners has shrunk once the ploughing started, and that's why we decided to convene this meeting. We are disgusted at what has happened. The common's been open heath for centuries, and now it is being destroyed. That's our view, and we want to hear what other people think, and what they think can be done about it. So, over to you." He sat down.

There was a long silence. Luke's father got to his feet again and spoke. "So who's going to speak first, and I would ask if you could say your name and where you come from before you make your point."

The silence was broken by a man at the back who stood up and, in a loud voice, said:

"My name is Ford and I live just a mile from the common. I've walked on the common for many years, usually with my dog, and recently I met Luke and put it to him that he should convene a public meeting, so I would like to thank him for doing that. I have to say that I'm appalled by what is happening with all this ploughing. Apart from anything else, the stench from all that manure is dreadful. It's the common, and it should be left alone for people to enjoy it as a public open space, simple as that."

There was a murmuring signifying general agreement. Another person stood up.

"I'm Mrs Coutts, and I live not far from the common. I visit the common often also with my dogs. It's a beautiful place, and sometimes when the heather and the gorse is in flower or early in the winter mornings when the frost is on the ground after a walk on the common I go home and write poems. They may not be much good, but they give me a lot of pleasure. I think this world is a beautiful place, but too much of it is being lost in one way or another. I can't believe that ploughing up the common can or should be allowed."

And another. "I am Flight Commander Porter, and I used to be based on the airfield during the war. Some of my colleagues were killed in accidents on the airfield during the war. They deserve to be remembered. I know that I have talked to young Luke about erecting a memorial where one of the fatal crashes had taken place, killing one of our best pilots. That area has now been ploughed up, which is a great shame. We do need to remember the sacrifices that were made on the common so that we can enjoy the freedoms we have today."

Luke looked at his father, and smiled. Then someone he did recognise stood up.

"I don't live near the common, and I only visit it during the summer. My name is Miss Harriet Crumble. I am sure many people here will have seen the small blue butterflies that flutter around the heather in the summer. This common supports the last remaining population of this butterfly in the whole of this region. You can go at least fifty miles in any direction from here and not find them. Why?" And now she raised her voice. "Because so many of the heaths around here have been destroyed. And now they're starting to do the same here. It's totally outrageous. Why are all you people," and here she looked round the room and spread her right arm wide to encompass everyone present and raised her voice, "letting this happen? Show some backbone, stand up for yourselves. Those who are responsible for this wanton destruction should be.......should be......well, I can't say but you can probably guess what I think. We, all of us, should have been aware that something like this was going to happen, but now we, all of us, have got to get it stopped." With that she sat down and many present started to clap to show their support.

There was a pause, and then Luke's father stood up and spoke.

"Many of you will have seen my lad Luke out on the common tending his cattle. We are the only commoners left who exercise their rights to put animals out to graze on the common. Others have rights, but they don't seem to bother any more. My father had the rights before me, and his father before him. Our family are commoners and have always been proud of it." Here his voice started to break. "It is who and what we are. We have always sought the best for the common. Seeing it being ploughed up.... just breaks my heart...." He had to stop and sit down. Luke put his arm around him. He had never witnessed his father speak with such emotion before. The meeting went very quiet.

Then someone else stood up.

"My name is Harris and I have a farm locally. People need to remember that only a few years ago this country was at war. One of the problems we faced then was that the country did not have enough food to eat. Once the war had ended the government had to introduce food rationing as there just was not enough food to go round. The government also made it clear that it wanted to see food production increased, so that we as a nation could grow more of our own food. That means bringing more land under the plough to grow crops. And we know that the population is increasing, more babies are being born and that there will be more mouths to feed. You can stand up and talk about how beautiful it all is, how pretty the butterflies are, how you can use it to graze a few cattle and so on, but at the end of the day you have to face a reality, that this country needs to produce more of its own food."

Voices could be heard muttering discontent, and someone else spoke.

"Yes but not here, not the common. You farmers have plenty of other land you can plough up, or learn how to get more produce off the land where you grow crops at the moment. You have other options. There's no need or justification to plough up the common."

"I'm just saying my point of view" responded Mr Harris, curtly. "People may disagree but this is a public meeting and I am entitled to express my opinion. This country needs to produce more food."

Another person got to her feet. "I'm Mrs Thompson and people will know me I expect as a local busybody as well as a farmer. I tend to get involved in all sorts of stuff locally. Personally, I wonder has anyone asked what is the legal basis for ploughing up a common. Is what is happening lawful? Who says you can just come onto the common with some tractors and other equipment and start ploughing and planting potatoes? Doesn't the government have a duty to protect these sorts of places?"

Another voice intervened. "I represent the owners of the common, and act as their agent. My name is John Biggar." Luke and his father recognised him as the man who visited their home and tried to buy their commoners rights. "In our view the work is completely legal and above board. The one commoner who exercises their rights still has sufficient space to graze his cattle, and this will be respected. The owners have a tenancy agreement with local farmers, Mr and Mrs Hughes, for them to cultivate the land and use it to grow crops as they chose. So not only are we enabling the land to provide more food for the nation, but also increasing local employment and benefitting the local economy."

A voice replied: "Who says you or someone else you claim to represent owns the common. It's common land, so nobody owns it."

And another voice: "I thought that, because it's common land, it was owned by all of us."

And another: "In my book the rights of ownership are with the local council." Someone else said they thought it was owned by the Crown.

Mr Biggar slowly, and somewhat wearily, got to his feet once more: "It is a generally held myth that commons are not owned. Practically all common land is owned by somebody, or some organisation. There are a few commons without any known owner, but this is not one of them. The word common refers to the fact that certain designated people have commoners rights attached to the title deeds of their properties. And as long as the rights of the active commoners are respected, the owner can do what they like with the land"

The level of disquiet rose, and people started to shout "That's preposterous" and "You cheating so-and-so." The meeting became more of a free-for-all, with a sense of orderliness being lost. Luke's father banged on the table and shouted for order, but to little avail.

The police constable got to his feet. "Ladies and gentlemen, I came here to prevent any breach of the peace. I thought that feelings may run high, so I would respectfully ask you to calm down." But this cut no ice with many present.

"So you say you don't own it, you're just representing the owners, so who the hell do you represent. Why aren't they at this meeting?"

"As you say, I am just a representative of the owners."

"Yes but who are the owners, and where are they?"

"I'm not at liberty to say."

"Well what's the point of having a discussion if all you can say is the owners can pretty much do what they like?"

"That's not my problem. The works will continue and that's all I'm prepared to tell you."

The meeting began to get even more rowdy. Miss Crumble stood up and went over to Mr Biggar, who had resumed his seat, and, standing directly in front of him, let rip.

"You appalling individual. You come here, no doubt taking a fat fee from your clients, and defend what to nearly everyone else feels to be indefensible. You call yourself an agent, and all you really are is an agent of destruction. All that is sacred, all that is beautiful, all that is enjoyed by so many people, all that provides a home for our native wildlife you seek to destroy." More applause from many present.

"Whatever I do and whatever my client does is within the law, and so we are fully justified in doing what we are doing. Perhaps you, all of you, would be so kind as to tell me one instance where we have broken the law, and I will be happy to discuss that with you. One aspect, that's all."

Silence. Then Luke's father spoke. "It's not just about the law, it's about what people feel is right and wrong, and people here feel that ploughing up the common is wrong. We may need to grow more food, but a line has to be drawn somewhere, and the common is the common, and not just another piece of farmland." Then, looking directly at Mr Biggar, he continued.

"You came to my house the other day with the Mr Hughes and tried to get me to surrender my commoners' rights by giving me £200. I don't know what people think of that, but it just seems that you see Luke and I as a nuisance to be got rid of."

A murmur of disbelief went round the hall, until one person stood up.

"In all my life I've never heard anything like it. You've been asked to betray your heritage for thirty pieces of silver. That's simply appalling."

"Hear, hear" could be heard as he sat down.

Mr Biggar continued. "We all live under the rule of law. If you want to campaign to get the law changed that is one thing, and you are all quite entitled to do that. But as the law stands we have done nothing wrong. You can talk about right and wrong until you're blue in the face but we have done nothing legally wrong."

More silence, as the mood of the meeting became more subdued.

Bill Westwood, who had been quiet up till now, got to his feet and began speaking loudly in his rasping voice. "I'm a commoner, you are destroying the common which I've known all my life, that is totally wrong to me and most people here. You say that the law is on your side, and you may be right about that, and maybe that's something that needs looking into more. But the fact remains that the views of the local people, the people who live around here, cannot be ignored. So you can take the comments you have heard tonight back to whoever sent you here, and let them know that if they don't change their minds about what they are doing there's only going to be more trouble laid at the door of cronies like you."

"I'm not going to just sit here and be insulted" said Mr Biggar.

"We're the ones who have been insulted by you being here" said another voice.

Mr Biggar quickly and haphazardly gathered together his papers and his briefcase, put his coat on without bothering to do up the buttons, walked out of the door muttering a hasty "Good night" as he left.

There was a long pause whilst people talked amongst themselves.

Luke's father stood up. "Ladies and gentlemen, please resume your seats." There was a general shuffling and murmuring as slowly people settled back down. He continued: "I'm not sure where we go from here. I suggest we go away and consider what we've heard tonight, all the different points of view before discussing matters any further. Those folk interested in what happens next I suggest they give their names and addresses to Luke so that we can contact them in the future."

But some people were not that happy to let matters rest there.

"We've got to fight this. We can't just lie down like lambs. We must not, must not let this matter end here." said one voice, to loud cheers of support.

"But we could be trying to fight an unwinnable fight. It sounds like they, the owners, whoever they are, hold all the aces, and just intend to do whatever they want to do. I don't want to be pessimistic, but I think we have to be realistic."

And with that people started to stand up and walk towards the door.

Soon Luke and his father were left alone in the hall. Luke didn't know what to think. He had come into the meeting with high hopes, but now felt it had achieved very little, as the ploughing was obviously set to continue.

"We tried, or rather you tried" said Luke's father. "Money talks and wins every time." He began stacking the chairs and put them against the walls of the hall, and Luke helped him.

Luke was sitting on the only chair that remained unstacked. He bowed his head and started to cry.

"Come on, that's enough" said his father, putting his arm round Luke's shoulders. "Let's go home."

They opened the door of the hall and pulled up the collars on their jackets as a winter storm had just arrived. Fat drops of rain were hammering down onto the road, swiftly followed by hailstones, all accompanied by huge flashes of lightening and the loud boom of thunder. The road was quickly turning into a stream in spate as Luke and his father made a dash for home.

5.

Visiting

Luke returned to the church to hand back the key to the hall. He was met at the church door not by the rector but by the young curate who was putting up some notices with drawing pins in the porch.

"You're the lad from the common who held the public meeting here last night? I'm sorry I couldn't come, as I would have spoken in support of you."

"Thanks for that" replied Luke, still feeling downcast.

"The rector is somewhere about. Ah, here he is" and with that the rector strode up through the churchyard and met the two of them at the church door.

"Come to give the key back? Mrs Bower is out, but you can just post it through the letterbox. I think the meeting was a bit of a disaster, wasn't it. Probably a foolish thing to do in the first place. You can't and shouldn't try to block progress."

"Well, I think Luke has got a good point. The common is a beautiful place, full of all sorts of creatures, all part of creation. I love to go there of an evening when the sun is going down and the day is coming to a close" replied the curate.

"All claptrap. We have to move with the times. It's no good harking back to some pastoral idyll, talking about beauty. The world moves on, there are mouths to feed, jobs to be created and money to be earned. Without it this place would just be stuck in poverty."

"But not the common, surely. The plants, insects and creatures that live there are wonderful, beautiful things, and we should not be destroying their home."

"I tell you when you have spent more time in the world you will come to see the error of your talk. Looking at things and thinking they are beautiful doesn't fill the stomachs of our parishioners."

"I think we must beg to differ, rector."

Luke realised he was just listening to the same arguments as he had heard the night before. There were two camps, and no sign of a meeting of minds, but he liked to hear what the curate said and it strengthened his own views.

"I'm off, but thanks anyway" and Luke posted the key through the letterbox, got on his bicycle and left them.

Winter turned into spring. Hundreds of tons of chicken manure, applied to enrich the sandy soil that was naturally poor in the nutrients and was needed to grow crops. All the local people complained about the stench and the flies. Fertilisers were also applied to improve the conditions for growing crops. Weeds emerged, but they were speedily dealt with by spraying with chemicals by means of a sprayer attached to a tractor. Then the tractor came back onto the common to plant potatoes, ridging up the bare soil.

Luke was still able to look after his few cattle as not all the common was ploughed, but he was pushed into smaller and smaller areas as more of the common disappeared under the plough. He looked on forlornly as the tractors went up and down destroying what he had loved. There were few birds to be heard or seen, fewer animals, fewer people. What had once been a place of beauty, a happy place where people could come and go freely enjoying the space and fresh air, a relaxed place where the butterflies fluttered and the birds sang, an historic place where people had died to save their country, was now becoming a place of industry and machinery, a place where the opportunity to earn some money for a few people was being seized at the expense of a long established way of life. Quite simply, Luke and his father felt that they had been trampled on.

Every day Luke would go out onto the common to tend his cattle, and he had plenty of time for thought. It was not the same for him for another reason, as Alina had gone. He felt sure she would have given him the push to fight harder to save the common. He knew that he had come to envy her confidence, her willingness to say things that perhaps he felt but was unable, or not confident enough, to voice. And her sense of daring, seeing much of what they did as an adventure. But would she have said the right thing, and not just something just for the sake of confronting people she did not like, reacting rather than thinking through the consequences? Whatever the truth was, Alina was no longer here, and so Luke felt he had to become more assertive, more able not to dissolve into tears as he had done when the ploughing has started and Miss Crumble the butterfly lady had turned on him, and more able to fight back. Not in the way Alina would, but in his own way, more thoughtfully. To do that he needed a plan, a path that would lead to the light where only darkness could now be seen.

One day whilst he was on the common by the land that had been ploughed his auntie Jean, who had spoken to him about what was being said by some people about his mother, approached him.

"Good morning Luke. How are you coping with your new neighbours, the tractor and the plough?"

"Not very well to be honest. I wish they would all disappear."

"Have you thought any more about what you can do about it?"

"Not really."

"It's not something anyone one person can begin to sort out on their own. Plenty of people spoke at the public meeting to say how appalled they were at what is happening to the common, and you need to speak to them individually now that a few weeks have past to see in a more practical way what can be done. And don't be so downhearted. All of us need to see if we can find a way. And the way will not be found if you just see yourself as a victim."

Luke thought briefly. "I don't understand that. How can I be anything else but a victim if they are taking away from me all that I have known and loved throughout my life?"

"A victim sees themselves as powerless, unable to do anything positive about what's affecting them. You need to find a way to stop seeing yourself as a victim and start, somehow, to gain a more positive view of yourself as someone who can exert some influence about what is going on here."

"I know that your husband is a farmer. As he's a farmer, why are you not in favour of the common being farmed? I thought all farmers were in favour of ploughing up more land, growing more crops and earning as much money as they can."

"No, not all of us. Perhaps there is a new breed, a more selfish breed, that just see it as a business, a means to get as much cash as they can. But others know deeper truths, such as that we should take into account the needs of other people, and other creatures that live on the land. The way these farmers are going about it with their new chemicals and ploughing up as much land as they can, gets all farmers a bad name. No more stewards of the countryside with the interests of wildlife and the public at heart, more like greedy people out for all the money they can get. There'll be enough food for everyone without ploughing everywhere up. And some land, such as the common, should never be ploughed up, but should be protected. I must be getting on, I've got my own work to do. Plenty to think about Luke." With that she began to walk away. But as she did so she saw a two people walking towards them, and she stopped.

"Good day" she said as they got nearer. "Mr and Mrs Hughes I believe."

"Yes indeed. And we know who you are, wife of a farmer still tied to the old way of doing things" replied Mr Hughes.

"Why didn't you come to the public meeting and hear people's views about what you are doing to the common?"

"We've got better things to do that listen to a load of people moaning. I hear it achieved absolutely nothing. We are here, we are using the land productively to the benefit of everyone by growing food for the nation, and here we stay, no matter what you and your supporters may say."

"I too farm along with my husband, as you know. We too grow crops for people to eat. That is not the issue. The issue is whether the common should be used in that way, or whether it is something different. Of course we need food, but there are other priorities too. The common has been unploughed for centuries before you came along, poor quality land not really fit for production unless heavily enriched with manures and fertilisers, best left alone. And there are many, many people who agree with us."

"At the end of the day to us it's just land, doesn't matter if it's the common or not. And land should be used to produce food for people to eat and jobs and an income for the likes of us, and that's the end of the matter as far as we are concerned."

Luke stood next to them, thinking that again he was listening to two polarised standpoints with no sign of any shared view, no agreed opinion and no prospect of anyone shifting. But more than that, he felt angry. He had listened to what the rector had said earlier, which had made him feel more disappointed than anything, but now he felt angry, and he knew why. It was not just the arguments about the common and what should happen to it, but what Mr and Mrs Hughes, and Mrs Hughes in particular, had said to him about his mother. As he stood there he could feel the anger growing inside. And he thought why should he bite his tongue and be polite? Why?

Luke walked up to Mrs Hughes until he stood just a couple of feet from her.

"You insulted my mother when Alina and I came round to see you, and you had no cause to do that. She would never have insulted you. So are you going to apologise?"

"Nothing she didn't deserve."

Luke was incensed. He went up to Mrs Hughes and looked her straight in the eyes. He was shaking with rage. He spoke with unconcealed anger.

"You do not do that, you have no right to do that, she was a far, far better person than you will ever be. And you can say what you like about your farming ideas, as it's the sort of character you are that matters more."

At this outburst Mr Hughes stepped forward and slapped Luke hard across his face. Luke recoiled from the blow, and rubbed his hand on his cheek. His anger had not diminshed

"There's absolutely no need for that, young man" said Mr Hughes. "We must be getting on, good day to you both."

"Bullies both of you" said Luke.

With that Mr and Mrs Hughes walked off briskly, and soon afterwards his aunt also left Luke, but not before telling him to call round to her house when he had finished tending his cattle.

It was a long walk to his aunt's farm, and he found her in the milking parlour. She greeted him and then invited him into her farmhouse, a comfortable family home with a relaxed feel to it. The entered the kitchen which was dominated by a large Aga. She started talking to Luke before he had sat down.

"Do you regret what you said today to Mrs Hughes."

"No. Maybe it was a bit strong, but he shouldn't have hit me."

"You're right, there's no reason to attack anyone physically, no matter what they might have said."

"Thanks."

With that Jean moved towards Luke and held him in her arms. Luke put his arms around her and his head on her shoulder.

"And for goodness sake stop behaving like a victim. Find the positive way forward - it's up to you to find the right path. I can't, nobody can, tell you what the right way is, you alone as a commoner have to find it. Have you thought any more about what we talked about the other day?"

"Yes" replied Luke. "It has helped, even though some of it hurt a lot, or maybe because it hurt quite a lot. I guess I will know one day what it feels like to love someone as she loved the pilot. But what it helped me realise more was how things are now with the common and my Dad and me, why people are putting around such a lot of hateful words to run us down."

Luke sat down and pondered for a while. He thought about the people his aunt had referred to who had spoken at the public meeting. Some were the same people he had been to see with Alina when they were trying to find out more about the pilot who had died, and others were different. It made him think how much better it would be if Alina were with him now. He missed her nerve, her confidence. She would have been able to rattle some cages to get things done. But now it was up to him, alone, with nobody to hide behind. He knew that his father could not offer much in the way of support as he still seemed so wrapped up in himself.

"There were several people at the meeting who were opposed to the ploughing. I could talk to them some more to find a way through all of this, to see how they might be able to help in some way."

"You see, Luke, there are some people whose views will not change. Mr and Mrs Hughes will not alter their opinions, so it's a waste of your time and theirs trying to persuade them otherwise, and more than that it just annoys them and makes them even more determined. You may get some pleasure from annoying them, but it does not advance your cause one jot. And what you've just said is a start, as you know there are people out there who feel the same way as you."

"Rather than a meeting, perhaps it would be better to talk to them one by one to see what can be done."

"And what you may find is that they each have a slightly different approach, a different interest and not just one single view, and that might be a good place to start. But remember, being angry, expressing hatred, will never get you or anyone else anywhere."

"We got people who were at the meeting to write down their names and addresses, so I can call round and speak to them one by one. That's where I'm going to start and see what come of it. There are some good people round about who do care for the common and I'll go and listen to what they can tell me."

"Let me know how you get on, and good luck" said his aunt as he disappeared through the door.

Luke decided to visit Flight Commander Porter first, as he had met him before and he had spoken so well at the public meeting. When he went to the house, he found him outside in his front garden, raking up leaves. The garden was kept immaculately.

"Young master Luke, hello."

"Hello. I was wondering if I might have a word with you about what you said at the public meeting the other day."

"As a matter of fact," replied the Flight Commander, leaning on his rake, "I've been having some thoughts about that myself. It grieves me to see a place where dedicated men and women, some of whom made the ultimate sacrifice, turned into a potato field. I decided to write a letter to the Ministry of Defence to see if there is anything they can do so that future generations will know that here, on this piece of common land, brave people fought for our freedom. I don't know if they can do anything, but it's worth a try."

"That's….that's….wonderful," said Luke, taken aback that the Flight Commander was prepared to do something to help. "Will you let me know what sort of reply you get?"

"I surely will, young man. These leaves are a damn nuisance, it's not that I mind them so much, it's that my wife likes everything kept nice and tidy."

With that Luke smiled and left him to his rake and his leaves. As he walked away he felt buoyed by the fact that someone was prepared to do something practical on their own accord. Who should be go and see next? Mrs Thompson.

Mrs Thompson lived in a large house on the side of the common few people visited, at the end of a road that was a dead end. She and her husband had lived there for many years and used to ride their horses on the common. Luke, feeling more confident, walked up to the oak front door and got hold of the big door knocker and gave it three loud knocks.

"All right, all right, I'm coming." said a voice from inside. "I'm not deaf you know."

Mrs Thompson opened the door. "Ah, it's you. I thought you might pop round. I suppose you want to know what I thought about the public meeting. Big waste of time that was. More of the common is getting ploughed up since then. I suppose you'd better come in."

She showed Luke into the kitchen, which was more than double the size of his kitchen at home. She took off her apron.

"You've timed that well, as the cake has just come out of the oven and the kettle is warming on the stove for some tea. No need to ask if you would like some I suppose?"

"I'd love some." replied Luke. The tea was poured into cups with saucers, and Mrs Thompson cut two slices of a victoria sandwich cake. "All made with eggs from our chickens and jam filling from raspberries from our garden" she boasted. "Now, what can I do you for?"

Luke had his mouth full of cake. He munched the cake as quickly as he could, took a gulp of tea and then put his hand over his mouth to stifle a burp and to prevent cake crumbs from exploding all over the kitchen before he started to speak.

"I know that at the meeting you were surprised, as we all were, that the common actually belonged to someone else, and that exactly who it belongs to remains a mystery. I wonder if you think that anything could be done to find out more."

"And why would you want to do this?"

"Well, if we could get in touch with the owners maybe we could ask them to stop ploughing."

"Fat chance." Mrs Thompson paused for a while. "But there might be some merit in just finding out who the owners are. If we knew perhaps we could start a dialogue with them, although maybe they would just tell us to go through their agents and that dreadful Mr Biggar. More cake?"

Luke thought for a moment, but, tempted though he was, he declined the offer.

"I'll do what I can to find out who owns the common" continued Mrs Thompson. "And I'll let you know what I find out."

"That's great" said Luke, with his eyes brightening. "Thanks so much."

As Luke left the house his spirits rose further. He had seen two people and they had offered to help. Next he should go and see Miss Crumble, the butterfly lady, but that would have to wait until tomorrow.

Luke knew where Miss Crumble lived, but it was a long bike ride away, so he set off early. As he got up from the breakfast table he told his father that he was going to visit Miss Crumble.

"What on God's earth are you going to see her for? They don't come any dafter than her."

"She may be able to help us save the common." replied Luke as he went to the back door.

"You be careful on those roads." shouted his father as Luke slammed the door behind him.

The journey took Luke about half an hour. Miss Crumble lived in a beautiful country cottage, with a small gate leading into a flower garden and a path leading to the front door, which was half smothered in a rambling rose. In summer the garden would be alive with the sound of bees and the scent of lavender. An old apple tree would be laden with fruit with sticks holding up some of the branches. Butterflies would be flying around all the flowers.

Luke propped up his bike on the wall outside the garden, opened the gate, walked up the path and knocked on the front door. It was answered by another woman, not Miss Crumble.

"Hello." said the woman, who smiled benevolently at Luke.

"I've come to see Miss Crumble. I want to talk to her about the common, where she comes to see the blue butterflies. I met her at the public meeting about the common recently."

"Oh yes, she talked to me about that. Well I'm afraid she's out at the moment, and won't be back for a while. I'm Joan. Do come in anyway and perhaps we can have a chat."

Luke entered the cottage and was shown into the lounge, which had a low ceiling with wooden beams running across and wooden props at various points holding up the ceiling. Along one wall was an inglenook fireplace with a few logs burning in the grate. The room had a very homely feel to it, with soft furnishings and lots of paintings and embroideries of country scenes on the walls.

"Do sit down" Luke sat down and half disappeared into one of the comfiest armchairs he had ever known. Joan sat down on a more upright wooden chair.

"I assume you're Luke, aren't you? Harriet has told me a lot about you and what has been happening on the common. We've been together for so many years and I have never known her so angry. She is so passionate about the butterflies. I like them too, but I don't spend all my time like her out and about identifying and counting them. I prefer to stay at home more and look after the garden and do my needlework and beadwork. You can see some of them on the walls here. What do you think of them?"

"I think they're very fine" replied Luke politely.

"Some of them have won prizes in competitions" Joan continued. "Harriet was particularly complementary about this one of the small blue butterflies resting on the pink heather she likes so much."

Luke looked at the framed embroidery, and he recognised it instantly as being something he had seen on the common many times.

"Harriet would have loved to have seen you, such a pity she's out. Can I help you at all?"

"Well I was really wondering if there was any way Miss Crumble could help us save the common. She came along to the public meeting and I know she has strong views about it all, but I wanted to see if she thinks there is anything practical we can do to stop the ploughing."

"Hmmm. That's very difficult, as I'm sure you realise. It's all such a shame. We live in such beautiful countryside and all some people want to do is destroy it to grow potatoes and make money. But Harriet is nothing if not a fighter and she loves a challenge. I'll tell her you called and perhaps you can meet up with her some other time."

"That would be good" replied Luke. He left the cottage not really knowing if he had made any progress or not.

As he rode back home took Luke realised he was going to pass the home of another person he felt it might be useful to visit. Bill Westwood was one of the commoners who had lived all his life by the common, and nobody knew it better.

Luke knocked on the front door. Immediately there was the sound of a dog barking aggressively, and the clanking of a chain as the dog tried to break free to confront him. There was no reply at the door, but soon he heard some footsteps and Bill Westwood appeared at a gate at the side of the house. He was dressed in a very worn tweed jacket, black trousers held up by baler twine, a neckerchief round his neck above an old striped shirt, a porkpie hat on his head and a walking stick in his hand.

"Come round the back here young master. Where's your girlfriend?"

"In Poland" replied Luke.

Luke followed him as he went inside through the back door and into a small room. He remembered the room from when he had visited before – bare floorboards, horse brasses, collars and harnesses on the walls which were stained yellow as a result of years of tobacco smoke. But now there was a bed in the corner, and Luke understood that he would have started to struggle to get upstairs in the evening. He got a tobacco tin out of his pocket and started to roll up a cigarette.

"This is my cabin. I just live and sleep in this room now. Like a cup of tea, with a drop of whisky in it?"

"I'm okay thanks" replied Luke.

Bill Westwood smiled showing big gaps in his teeth and then laughed as he said this, his voice harsh and gravelly, belying his friendly manner towards Luke.

"I remember who you are. You're Luke the son of the chap whose lived by the common for nearly as long as me. Aye, I know thee. You keep those few cattle on the common. And good for you, I say, the only commoner whose keeping the old ways going. I used to keep some animals on the common but those days are gone for me. Sometimes I used to take my two horses on there to have a bit of grazing but even that's too much for me now. Especially since those bastards started ploughing it up. Totally against the law if you ask me, but is there anyone who cares about that? I enjoyed the public meeting, not that it got us very far. Good to see that agent chappie get a taste of the views of people round here. He got in a right huff before storming out. Now then, what can I do you for?"

"Well, I was thinking that maybe the people who care about the common could try to see what they might do to save it."

"The common is the common, and always will be, no matter what some people do with it. I know a solicitor chappie who lives not far from here and some nights I meet him in pub round the corner, The Fox, and I can have a word with him about the legal side of what's going on. You would have thought our commoners' rights would be protected by the law, but the law is a funny thing, open to many different interpretations. Most people think the law is clear as day, but anyone who deals with it knows it's usually far from clear cut. And then there are the lawyers, who can talk for hours on end and convince people that black is white and white is black. I'll see what advice he can give, but don't hold your breath."

"Thanks" said Luke as he made his way to the door.

"Don't mind the dog." Luke warily negotiated his way round from the back door to ensure he stayed beyond the reach of the chained animal.

Luke remembered seeing the local lord of the manor, known roundabout as just Sir Geoffrey, when he and Alina had visited the pilot's grave, and the thought occurred to him that there would be no harm in paying him a visit. He knew that some time ago he would not have had the confidence to do this, but he now felt that he was better able to say things to people he would have shied away from saying before. Everyone knew where the manor house was, on the outskirts of the village near the church, hidden from view by a sweeping drive bordered by shrubs and large sweet chestnut trees. When Luke arrived at the large wooden front door he pulled the bell and the door was opened by Sir Geoffrey himself, wearing a tweed jacket and tomato-red corduroy trousers, accompanied by two sleek greyhounds.

"Are you going to try and sell me something, because if that's the case you can bugger off now" said Sir Geoffrey whilst looking sternly at Luke.

"No, nothing like that. It's just that I'm one of the commoners and I'd like to know your views about what's happening on the common with all the ploughing."

Sir Geoffrey paused for a moment before replying. "I see. Let's go for a walk along the terrace and have a chat about it, shall we?"

Sir Geoffey's greyhounds followed him as he stepped outside onto the gravel terrace and Luke walked along next to him.

"I suppose you're right to be upset about it in one way. I can understand that ploughing and growing crops doesn't do much for your commoners' rights. But here's the thing – you're the only commoner exercising their rights, and when you stop there will be nobody there. And then what happens to the common? Well it won't be a common anymore, only in name, so you might as well turn it into something useful and productive. And then what's the point of calling it a common anyway, you might as well get it declassified so that it becomes just a piece of farmland. It's the same all round here, with various places called such-and-such a heath, but all the heathland has been turned into arable farmland to grow crops or pasture. The names still survive, but the reality is totally different. That's the way the world is going – more people need more food. In a way, though, it saddens me."

"Why's that?"

"Well, my family's association with the common goes back generations. In fact, you can probably assume that my ancestors some centuries ago owned the common, allowing some families to turn out their grazing animals there and collect brushwood as it was poor quality land, not suitable for agriculture. And then the common was sold to someone else, most likely to pay for upkeep of this huge house or to pay the taxman death duties, and was probably sold on again and again, so heavens alone knows who owns it now. I've absolutely no idea. And now the common is no longer what it once was, and it's no use pretending that it is. Times change, and the common has to change with the times. And it's really lost its function as a common, so I think the present owners, whoever they are, should be left to do whatever they see fit, and furthermore it should no longer be termed common land.

"But you've just told me it's part of your heritage, as it is part of my heritage, although in a different sense. Your family may have once owned the common, my family still has rights on the common, so we share an interest. Why can't you accept that we also have a shared duty to protect and look after the common?"

Sir Geoffrey paused. "Come indoors."

Sir Geoffrey shows Luke into the dining room of the house, which was mainly taken up by the longest table he had ever seen, made out of mahogany and French polished so that Luke could clearly see his face in it. It made him think of a film he had once seen, a comedy, which in one scene had the lord and lady of the manor sitting at opposite ends of a huge table, with the butler walking up and down from one end of the table to the other with the breakfast marmalade.

Sir Geoffrey got Luke to sit down next to him and he opened an old photograph album containing black and white photographs of the common, families enjoying picnics, people riding horses, children with smiles on their faces.

"My father was a keen photographer and he used to go onto the common to record the scenes there. I would like to think that it could be preserved somehow, it's just that I don't see how."

"Well, I'm determined to find a way. Would you support us if we could find a way to keep it safe and stop all the ploughing?"

"I might I suppose, for the sake of my father and the generations of my family."

Luke felt elated by this seeming change of heart, or he thought maybe not a change of heart but Sir Geoffrey realising where his heart lay. For the first time he had witnesses someone change their stance rather than becoming more entrenched in their opinion. Strange bedfellows him and Sir Geoffrey, he thought.

"Is it all right if I get in touch again, when I'm clearer about what we could do?"

"By all means. You're a fine young man, Luke" and Sir Geoffrey shook Luke firmly by the hand.

Luke got on his bicycle once more and headed for home, his heart lifted by what he perceived as some chinks of light in his struggle to save the common. The country lanes were generally quiet and the sunshine added to Luke's more positive mood. Apart from the occasional car there was very little traffic on the road, until Luke could see a tractor approaching. As it got nearer the noise increased, and just before it came alongside Luke it swerved into his path and collided with the side of his bicycle, with the result that Luke came off and fell into a ditch on the roadside with the bicycle on top of him. As the tractor sped away he could hear the sound of a man laughing above the noise of the tractor engine. It all happened so quickly that Luke was unable to see who the man was, but he knew that it wasn't an accident. Luke was not badly injured, just dazed, with a few scratches and grazes, but his bicycle was badly damaged. He walked the rest of the way home, pushing his bicycle with its bent wheels along as best he could.

6.

Interlude

S pring and warmer weather came on the common. Flight Commander Porter had never really retired from the Royal Air Force. To this day he spent much of his time reading through old papers, looking at old photographs, attending reunions with old colleagues and remembering those who gave their lives in conflict. To him the Royal Air Force was not just a job, something he had been paid to do, but something that defined his whole life, something that was bigger than himself, that gave him meaning and purpose. He was not a religious man in the accepted way in which the phrase is used, but to him the Royal Air Force was like a religion in the way it formed the basis of what he valued in life and what he did with his time now that he was retired.

He would often be seen walking on the common, and he still wore his Royal Air Force cap as he did so. Sometimes he would think he was hearing planes revving their engines before take-off, especially when he walked there in the evenings. He would like to walk down the whole length of the runway, stopping every now and then as a particular memory of a particular flight or incident entered his mind. Leaning on his walking stick he would pause and look around him, re-living whatever it was that had come back to him. More than anything he wanted to see those memories preserved so that, when he was gone, younger people would also have reason to stop and reflect on the courage, the comradeship and the sacrifice that he had witnessed.

The ploughing up of much of the common had disturbed him greatly. He saw it as a way of trying to erase those memories, trying to say that all that is to be forgotten now and buried, literally. The runway was still there, along with the old control tower, but he wondered for how much longer before they were demolished. What would then be left to tell the story of what had taken place here?

He found it difficult to walk over the soft ploughed ground, and although he was aware that maybe some people would say it was something he shouldn't do as he was compacting the soil and thus harming the crops, he nevertheless felt he was entitled to walk wherever he wanted on the old airfield. In many ways he saw it as belonging to him and his colleagues, and that therefore he had certain rights to it, in much the same way as the commoners had rights on the land. One spot he felt drawn to visit was the site where the bomber plane had crashed, killing Flight Lieutenant Jim Craig. It was some way off the runway, near a small copse of trees. He recalled chairing the enquiry and learning how the pilot had ensured that all the crew had managed to disembark safely before the crash, the terrible injuries the pilot had suffered and how his death had affected the whole squadron. He would stand there on ground close to what was now a potato field, take off his cap and bow his head.

Back home he would tell his wife that there should be some sort of memorial on the spot where the plane had crashed. He did not know what sort of memorial, but he felt that something permanent should be there to mark what had happened. Maybe it should be a small stone plaque, maybe an obelisk. Maybe it should commemorate not just the pilot but also all those who served here during the war.

He wrote letters to the government and the Royal Air Force about it. Each time the same reply came back, that he would have to obtain the permission of the owner of the land. He knew that it was common land, and, as he thought that there was no owner, he persisted with his letters and eventually arranged for an official from the Royal Air Force to come and meet with him on site.

"Here's the spot where the bomber plane crashed, and the pilot sustained injuries that led to his death" he explained to the official.

The official looked round about. He could see a few cattle grazing in the distance, and the potatoes growing in their rows. He knew that various places across the country had requested some sort of monument to aircraft personnel who had lost their lives, and this was just one more. He had listened to so many tales of heroism that he felt he was getting immune to yet another one.

"Without some sort of permission from the owner..."

"But I don't know who he owner is" interrupted the Flight Commander.

"And because of that I'm not convinced we can take this any further. We can't just go round putting up memorials willy-nilly wherever we like, it has to be done with due process. I can appreciate how much it means to you, but there's nothing further I can do in this instance. If you will excuse me I've got other matters, other sites to look into, so I am going to bid you good day."

With that the meeting was over and they walked off the common together in silence. The Flight Commander went home and was asked by his wife how the meeting had gone.

"Completely useless individual. No direct experience of the war himself. Bureaucracy gone mad. Feel like I'm banging my head against a brick wall."

"Perhaps it's time to stop trying to get your memorial."

"Never. Never." And with that he went outside to relieve his frustration by mowing the lawn.

******

Bill Westwood knew that he could meet his solicitor friend any night of the week in The Fox. As he entered the pub he immediately went over to where his friend was sitting and, after buying a round of drinks, he began with a question.

"So, you will have seen all the ploughing that's been going on across much of the common. What's your take on it from a lawyer's point of view?"

"The law relating to common land is bloody complicated, that's my view" came the reply, and they both started to laugh. He continued "Do you want me to give you an absolute definitive answer regarding the legality or otherwise of the ploughing, because if that's what you're after you might as well ask the chap that's serving behind the bar. I know how strongly you feel about the moral rights and wrongs of what is going on, but you know that the law is a completely different beast compared to that. We lawyers can easily make things so complicated, dress everything up in a language that your ordinary man on the bus cannot in any way comprehend, refer to strange historic cases that may have set a precedent a hundred years or so ago, get dolled up in funny costumes and wigs, and that all ends up a million miles from someone looking at the ploughing and thinking 'That doesn't seem right to me'.

"I know all of that. But just give me some ideas of the legal arguments that might be put forward, both for and against. What I'm trying to get to is whether there's any point in us hiring a lawyer to start a case, or whether going down that road would just be pouring money, which we would struggle to come by anyway, down the proverbial drain."

"OK, I'll tell you how I see it as a lawyer, and not just a lawyer who's touting for business and encouraging you to start proceedings, but an independent opinion." He took a long drink from his pint glass before continuing. "Firstly, the case for the plaintiff - in this instance you. You have rights of common on the land that are attached to the title deeds of your property.

These rights exist for ever, in perpetuity as a lawyer like myself would say. The rights were established centuries ago when the lord of the manor allowed certain people to use his land as it was too poor agriculturally to grow any crops. It was often referred to as waste land on account of this. The rights include the right to turn out grazing animals onto the common. All that sets out the background, which we can expect that the other side, the defendant, in this case the owners of the common, to agree on.

"Now we come to the more contentious bit. The owners have ploughed up the common, but not all of it, just most of it. They have left you enough land that is still suitable for grazing. You can still exercise your rights there if you chose to, as I believe one individual still does."

"That's young Luke and his dad" interjected Mr Westwood.

"But what if you intended to turn out cattle, ponies or whatever onto the common? Would there still be sufficient grazing available? And what if not just you but all the commoners who don't exercise their rights at present decide to turn out their animals, if they have any? Does it matter that people don't exercise their rights now but might or could in the future, or can the owner just carry on doing what he or she wants regardless?"

"Several questions there, but no bloody answers!"

"That's the point. There are no definitive answers. The matter has never been decided in a Court of Law, there is no legal precedent, so we just don't know. The only way to find out is to take the matter to court. And then the judgement might go one way or the other in a lower court, which would mean that whoever lost could appeal the judgement to a higher court, and again if that judgement overturned the original decision or whatever the matter could go to an even higher court."

"Sounds like it could take years, and then there's the small matter of the cost of paying for the lawyers, not just solicitors like yourself but barristers as well I suppose. And I know full well that they don't come cheap, to put it mildly. We are talking about thousands and thousands of pounds."

"That's right. In my view the issue is finely balanced between the commoners and the owners, it could go either way, and it would take a huge amount of time and a vast amount of expense to get a definitive answer. Have you ever read Bleak House by Charles Dickens? It's a story of how an interminable legal case regarding a family inheritance lasts many, many years, and how the legal fees of all the lawyers eventually drains the financial resources of the individual plaintiffs, eventually robbing them of not just their rightful inheritance but also their health and happiness. Even if you are successful you could end up with a crippling bill for legal costs. Sometimes you take a matter to court at your peril, no matter the size of the injustice you are seeking to redress."

"And the rights of people to walk on the common, to enjoy the fresh air and the wildlife?"

"The same arguments apply."

"It's what I expected you to say. There's no way we should be taking the matter through the courts, and we will just have to find another way to save the common. Bastards the lot of them."

******

Mr and Mrs Hughes regularly attended the Sunday morning church service conducted by the rector. They always sat in the same pew and enjoyed a conversation with the rector in the parish hall once the service had ended. Sir Geoffrey and his family were also there, and an entire pew at the front of the nave had been reserved for the family for several generations.

On one Sunday the rector preached a sermon based on a particular text from the bible, the parable of the talents, praising those that use their gifts to the fullest. He used the sermon to congratulate those who, as he saw it, advanced the good of humankind by spending their time wisely to produce benefits for everybody. He took the matter further by castigating those that stood in the way of such endeavours or were trying to prevent such people from exercising their talents, and spelt out for special commendation those who sought to increase the amount of land that could be used profitably to produce food. Mr and Mrs Hughes sat in their pews with a feeling of self-righteous smugness.

After the service the rector and the congregation adjourned to the parish hall for tea and biscuits. Mr Hughes congratulated the rector on a first-class sermon.

"Well" replied the rector "I was only referring to what is written in the scriptures. I expect that you are quite familiar with the text anyway. By the way, is everything going well on the common?"

"As well as can be expected. We've had very little trouble from the locals apart from a bit in the beginning. We look set for a reasonable crop of potatoes."

"I am pleased to hear it." And with that the rector moved away to talk to some of his other parishioners. Mr and Mrs Hughes meanwhile quickly drank their cups of tea and left.

The rector was then taken to one side by Sir Geoffrey, who had seen him talking to Mr and Mrs Hughes and had taken exception to the message the rector had tried to put across in his sermon.

"Rector, you would be best advised not to make points that some may take as supporting what is taking place on the common. We are not all in agreement with it, and to bend the parables to suit a particular point of view is ill-advised."

The rector was stuck for words for a moment, but then said "I was only trying to illustrate a point that would have some resonance with the congregation."

"It did have plenty of resonance with me, but not in the way you suggested. Some people use their talents, if that's what you call them, in ways that are not right. I've been thinking about this a lot recently, and have come to alter my views about what's happening on the common. What you term progress may actually be more a case of destroying what has continued to exist for generations, and has become part of our heritage. I know that you don't come from these parts, so you need to be very careful about what you say about what goes on round here. To acquaint yourself a little more understanding about the history, traditions and the nature of this area instead of just blindly going on about progress as if it were God would be no bad thing. Think on it." And with that Sir Geoffrey strode off. The rector was lost for words, not daring to cross swords with Sir Geoffrey.

******

Jean Williams remembered very well the time Luke's mother, her sister, had died. She used her position as a children's social worker to speak to the headteacher of his school and arrange for Luke, than aged just eight years, to have some time off school then, and to make sure the other children treated Luke sensitively when he returned. Initially Luke had been very quiet when he came back to the school, and although he soon fitted in with his friends again, what had happened made him more serious. At times when she looked at him Jean could see that he was deep in thought, as he was by nature an introverted child.

Her main interest outside of her work and the family farm was history, and she often would walk on the common with her dog, seeing if she could find anything of historical note. On one occasion she found pieces of a bronze age cinerary urn and the human bones they once contained, over three thousand years old. When the ploughing had started she was keen to walk over those areas to see if there were any historical artefacts that the plough had brought to the surface. All she found, however, were rusty old tin cans and pieces of old boots.

She loved her dog, a spaniel called Maisie. During the spring and summer she would keep Maisie on a lead so as not to disturb the skylarks that nested on the ground amongst the heather and the grasses, but at other times Maisie would be free to run around and chase the rabbits. She often stopped to talk to other people out on the common walking their dogs, and all of them spoke disapprovingly of the ploughing, shaking their heads. But all of them were somewhat fatalistic about it, saying that, although they disliked it, it was progress and had to be accepted, or that it was better to see the land brought into agricultural production considering the position of the nation after the war. None of them seemed of a mind to do anything about the changes that were taking place apart from shrug their shoulders. This left Jean feeling quite shocked, as she struggled to understand how people could be accepting of a change that was going to deprive them of something they enjoyed. "We'll just have to find somewhere else to go and walk the dog" was the general response if she suggested they might actually try and do something to stop the ploughing.

Back at home Jean talked to her husband about the common. He encouraged her to do something as he could perceive that she felt strongly about what was happening, and was disappointed by what she felt was a lack of interest or support to do anything about it. Her husband told her that what was needed was some leadership, someone to be a figurehead for a campaign to save the common, and then others might be more willing to lend their support. Jean agreed, and she knew who that person should be.

******

Luke's father became reluctant to venture out onto the common, asking Luke to do all the work tending the cattle. He was very much aware that the heritage of his family back through generations that had lived in the cottage was being obliterated. His family had always been part of the common, as if it were a limb. Now that limb was dying, and he expected it to be completely dead in a few years' time. In short, he was in mourning, a mourning based on the expectation of a death. He blamed himself for letting down the generations that had preceded him, as it was on his watch that the destruction of the common had commenced. He became a sad figure, and those who knew him could see him withdrawing more and more into himself.

Amongst his acquaintances were Alina's parents. With Alina away in Poland her mother turned her attention to others, including Luke and his father. She always recalled how Luke's father had been one of the very few people who had welcomed them into the camp some years ago, and, as she could sense the hurt that people like him were now experiencing, she now felt it was time to repay them for the kindness that had been bestowed on them. She called round and found Luke's father sitting at the kitchen table alone as Luke was outside tending the cattle. She brought with her some beans and peas from her small vegetable plot, and a bottle of homemade mead, a traditional Polish drink that her husband made using the honey from their two beehives, as well as a jar of honey which could be used as a substitute for sugar in tea. Luke's father offered to open the bottle of mead straight away, and stood up to fetch some glasses, but Alina's mother told him not to, but to save it so that he and Luke could enjoy it together.

Luke's father was very appreciative of the gifts, especially as he was not in the habit of receiving anything from anybody. The conversation between the two of them was a little stilted, owing to her poor knowledge of English and his reserved manner. He asked if they had heard at all from Alina, and the reply was that no letter had arrived, which was to be expected as it would take at least a few weeks for a letter to come in the post. In turn, Alina's mother asked how Luke was, and if he was missing

Alina. Luke's father replied that he thought he was, although he didn't show it. Alina's mother invited Luke's father round to their abode for lunch one day, and that made him look up suddenly as if startled, as nobody had invited him out like that for many years. He said he would like to come, and she told him to bring Luke with him next Wednesday.

Luke and his father duly knocked on the door of the nissen hut on the Wednesday lunchtime. Luke was clutching a tin of biscuits as a gift. Inside they sat down to a Polish meal of pork stew with vegetables and sourdough bread, followed by a cheesecake topped with a fruit jelly. Afterwards they were offered Polish sweets, and, just Luke's father, a shot glass of Polish vodka. Luke had a sip of it, and started coughing and splutterling. When it was time to go Luke's father told his hosts that it had all been delicious, although not quite what he was used to, and he went on to say, with some emotion, that nobody had showed him such kindness for a long time. Luke joined in with his thanks, and Alina's mother went up to him and kissed him on both cheeks.

******

Harriet Crumble had been a keen lepidopterist for practically her whole life. She was familiar with various places in the county where she could find different species of butterflies and moths, some of them woodlands, some wildflower meadows, some old quarries, some roadside verges, some bogs and marshes, some high hillsides with rocky outcrops. She would often be seen out and about with a butterfly net in one hand and a notebook in the other to record her sightings. But her favourite place was the common and its heathland, and the rare blue butterfly it supported.

She was a woman of boundless energy, not only physical energy in clambering around some fairly inaccessible places in search of butterflies but also the energy to inspire other people. She formed a local group of like-minded people who cared about the wildlife in the county, and in particular butterflies, which she chaired. The group met regularly to share information about sites they had visited and different species they had seen. Miss Crumble herself typed up a newsletter on an old typewriter, made by the American company Royal, that one of the group had given to her, using just her index fingers as they bounced up and down on the heavy keys. Once she had typed it she gave it to another member of the group who took it into the nearby town for photocopying on the very latest machine, called a Xerox, so that everyone had a copy.

As well as meetings and a newsletter Miss Crumble arranged site visits for the group. These were usually all day affairs, with Miss Crumble's Austin A40 car taking as many passengers as could be squeezed in along with some other vehicles, although this sometimes meant that the cars struggled going uphill. It was not unknown for group members to have to get out and push, with Miss Crumble staying in the driver's seat and shouting encouragement. When they arrived at the designated place they would spread out, some with nets and some without, some with cameras and some not, and try to identify what they saw. One member of the group would have a notebook so that everything was recorded, the particular butterfly species and their number, as well as other insects, creatures and wildflowers of interest. Miss Crumble's partner Joan came with the group, although she preferred to sketch the landscape rather than chase after the butterflies, and she would use the sketches later at home to produce watercolour paintings.

Members of the group were generally of an advanced age, with just one or two younger enthusiasts, and often after eating their sandwiches at lunchtime they would stretch out their legs whilst sitting on a grassy bank, and the sound of group snoring was soon to be heard. This gave Miss Crumble the opportunity to get together the younger members and talk to them about how to identify different species of butterflies and moths, good field guides they could suggest as Christmas or Birthday presents and equipment such as nets and pots, and magnifying lenses for some of the more difficult species. She cautioned everyone against pinning dead butterflies and displaying them in glass cabinets, or worse still selling them, saying this was so unnecessary and cruel – the butterflies should be allowed to live their natural lives without being predated by humans. Then Miss Crumble would summon up the rest of the group to resume the challenge to find as many different species as they could, especially rare ones, before the drive home.

Of course Miss Crumble would often talk to the group about the small blue butterfly on the common, and it was only by visiting other heathland sites in the region that she was able to establish that the common was the only place where this particular butterfly survived. Once the ploughing started, however, she became so angry and saddened by what had happened that she found it difficult to visit the common as frequently as she did previously.

******

Summer 1944. The airfield dominated the common, with planes, vehicles and people all active day and night. There were some corners of the common, however, that were not part of the airfield, that were neither concreted over or mown, and it was on these parts that the wildflowers, the butterflies, the trees and the birds could still be found, exiled from their usual more extensive home.

Sometimes after the school had finished for the day, and with Luke of an age when he could make his own way home, Luke's mother liked to walk onto the untouched areas of the common. Sometimes she would dreamily stroll through the long grasses, letting her hands brush against the flowers and the seed heads of the grasses, disturbing the insects as she went. At other times she would find somewhere to sit, either on the grass or on a fallen tree. She was always alone, time she valued just to be with herself and let the worries and concerns that the day had brought gently drift away. It was during one of the times, whilst she was sitting on an old tree trunk, that she met a pilot based at the airfield.

"Can you hear the bird singing in the willow tree?" he said as he approached her, still wearing his uniform. "It's a willow warbler, the sound of summer. Beautiful, isn't it."

"Yes, I suppose it is" she replied, taken aback by the directness of someone she had never met before.

"A gentle song of a few notes descending in pitch and fading away into nothingness."

"I'm afraid I'm not very good at identifying all the different bird songs."

"Well, if you can spare a few minutes, why don't I teach you some of them?"

"If you like, although whether I shall remember them all is another matter."

By this time he was standing next to her.

"Let's walk over to the copse and find out what's there." He offered her his hand as she got up, her small hand fitting neatly into his.

"Now, can you hear a different song, a series of short notes, slowing down at the end. We have to wait to see if he sings again." The bird sang. "That's it, did you hear it."

"I did, but I've no idea what it was."

"A yellowhammer. If you look on top of the gorse bush over there you can see it perched on top."

There was a long pause as they waited for the bird to sing again. She looked at him and smiled. "Do you think it's going to sing again?"

"It will" and as the pilot finished these words the bird sang once more.

She looked at him and smiled again. "I really know very little about birds, but I do know some of the wildflowers here on the heath. But I'd better be getting back and prepare tea for my young son."

"So tomorrow you can show me your wildflower knowledge?"

"Maybe" she replied, still smiling, and as she walked off the common back home she was surprised how meeting a total stranger had not felt at all awkward, but rather something unique. She realised that they both clearly shared an appreciation of the creatures that made the common their home, their beauty in both sight and sound. She thought it was something she should like to take further tomorrow.

The next day they met at the same spot. The pilot was not in uniform this time, but Luke's mother had put on her favourite summer dress and tied her hair back neatly.

"So are you going to tell me the names of the plants that grow here?" said the pilot.

"Come over here and kneel down. Look down here amongst the fine grasses and you can see a plant with tiny white flowers. It's called Shepherd's Cress. And over here is a plant with its blue flowers held higher on a single stem. It's called Sheep's Bit, and it's very popular with the bees. Many local people call it Blue Buttons." She gently cupped the flower between her fingers.

"I have walked over here many times but never noticed these plants before."

"The names tell their own story. Maybe the plants are palatable to sheep, which at one time would have grazed here."

"So you are giving me a lesson not just in the names of the plants but their meaning. I'm very impressed."

"Sometimes I bring my class of school children here and we sit on the grass and I teach them the names of the plants. I tell the children not to pick the flowers, though they like to do this. I think it's important for them to know the names of the plants, for this place is their common and the more they know about it the more they will appreciate it and look after it."

"I didn't know that you are a teacher. Tell me more about what you do."

"Why do you want to know that?" she said, smiling and almost laughing. "Well, it's a very small school, which is not a bad thing as we can give the children more individual attention. You get to know the children very well. They are just starting out on life so it's important to open their eyes to the world around them in all sorts of ways, and to make them curious about everything, to allow them to ask all sorts of questions. We never really stop learning if you remain curious, at least I don't."

"Very true. What's this one called?" said the pilot, pointing to another flower. As he did so he put his hand gently on her shoulder.

"It's Bird's-foot Trefoil, or bacon and eggs on account of its red and yellow flowers. Now you really should have known that one as it's a common wildflower."

"I just wanted you to tell me" he replied, with his hand still on her shoulder, stroking it.

She stood up and straightened her dress. "Well, that's your lesson over for today. I must be getting home I suppose. Here we are spending time together and I don't even know your name."

"It's Jim. And yours?"

"Linda."

Over the next few weeks they met often on the common, usually after the school day was finished. She made him talk about his life as an RAF pilot, and he listened as she told him about her daily life in the classroom. At other times they talked about what they saw around them on the common. The pilot brought his binoculars so that they could see the birds more clearly, and Linda teased him that he wanted to be able to fly with their agility. She pointed out the butterfly lady with her net.

"That woman is often here, chasing after the butterflies. Some people mock her and call her the Bug Lady, but really if you talk to her and listen to her passion for the common and the blue butterflies you realise she is talking a lot of sense. She knows the importance of insects and the places where they live to our own health and well-being, unlike so many people."

The pilot told her what he knew about her. "On the airfield she is often a talking point, as we see her in the distance away from the runways and the run-offs. Some of the crews do think she is crazy, but it's a reminder of peacetime, and the peace we are fighting for – to be left in peace to pursue whatever it is that we feel strongly about. And she's a good woman, as once she turned up at the mess with a cake for all the crews after we had suffered a loss. She didn't say much, but it was such a welcome gesture to know that someone locally cared about us."

"You must have fears not just for your colleagues but also for yourself. It must be very dangerous, even though it is just training flights. I often hear the planes fly over at night and think it may be you, and then stay awake fearing that you will not make it back to the airfield. Darling, please take care." Linda's eyes filled with tears as she said these words.

"I will, of course. Of course it's dangerous, more so for those flying missions over enemy territory, but we just have to go through with it and hopefully come out unscathed, as a nation, as a squadron and as individuals. I don't want you to worry" he replied as he stroked her hair with his hand.

Linda smiled as she took hold of his hand and kissed it. She loved hearing him talk with understanding, affection and intelligence, and she knew this was in contrast to her life at home with her husband. She was becoming closer to him, loved being with him, looked forward to when they would be spending time together, if only for a short while. And afterwards she would be filled with a feeling of being alive that she had not experienced before, and then she knew that she had fallen in love. It was not long before he placed his arm around her waist and gently pulled her towards him. They kissed, tenderly, and he laid her down on the grass.

Of course she was frightened that her husband would find out, and how hurt he would be, so she tried to keep it a secret. The only person she told was her sister, Jean, whom she knew would be able to keep it to herself, and when she mentioned it Jean cautioned her about the dangers involved in seeing someone else in such an open situation.

"People will see the two of you together and form their own opinions, and share those opinions with others. And eventually it will get back to you, people will make cruel remarks or insinuations, either to your face or behind your back. Things might even be said to Luke."

Linda bit her lip. "I know, and I would do anything to protect Luke. But I just want to be with him all the time. It's what I am, what I am meant for, I can't describe it any other way. Where else can we meet except on the common?"

Jean wondered if it might be better if she offered her farm as a meeting place for the couple, but with all the farm workers around this would be no less public. People could and would see them together and draw their own conclusions.

"You know that word about all of this will get back to Luke's father. Imagine how hurt he will be. And as for Luke, if he was to be teased...."

Word had got back to Luke's father. He knew, and he also understood. He understood that Linda had found someone else, and he understood that he had to protect Luke from any gossip. Between himself and Linda there had been no conversation about the pilot, as in fact they had stopped conversing about anything that could involve any emotion several years previously, and the words they exchanged were just about practical day-to-day arrangements.

"I know. I don't want it to be like this. Sometimes I think about just running away, anywhere."

Jean herself felt torn, torn between supporting her younger sister, as they had always been close, and censuring her for what she was doing.

"Have you ever been in love, so deeply in love that nothing else really matters any more apart from being with that one person? As though you had discovered another world that had previously been a locked room to you?" Linda asked.

Jean chose not to answer. "Just be careful, very careful, where all this might lead. I will always be here for you if you need me."

But Linda never needed her again, and they never met again, as within a week she had died suddenly from an infection. On her way to meet the pilot one day she was in a rush as she had had to stay behind to help one of her pupils after lessons had finished. She decided to take a short cut across part of the airfield by climbing over a barbed wire fence. As she did so one of the barbs caught her lower leg through her dress, making a deep cut and leaving a piece of material snagged on the fence.

"Oh, why does there have to be a fence here, there never used to be one" she said to herself as she hurriedly tore a piece off her dress and bandaged the wound to stop the flow of blood. The rest of her dress covered the wound so that nobody would be able to see it. She never went to seek medical help to have the wound properly and hygienically dressed as she feared that people might start spreading gossip about how her leg came to be cut. And she paid for that decision with her life.

Within a couple of days she had taken to her bed, feeling unwell, and then she became feverish, taking fast, short breaths. Luke spent time with her initially, sitting on the edge of the bed and telling her what he had done at school that day, but as her condition worsened Luke's father told Luke it was better that she was left alone. She did not want the doctor initially, but as her health deteriorated and she started to become delirious, shouting incoherently and drifting in and out of consciousness, her husband insisted and the doctor came. He examined her in the morning and diagnosed a case of blood poisoning and arranged for an ambulance to take her to hospital urgently. The eight year old Luke stood by the door as the ambulance crew carried his mother out of the house on a stretcher. His father told him to stay at home and not to worry as she was going to get better and be home again soon. When she arrived at the hospital she had deteriorated further, and the hospital consultant told Linda's husband that the only way to save her would be to amputate her leg. Her husband was in a complete state of shock. He was unable to make up his mind initially, but then gave his consent. She died on the operating table.

The funeral was held, attended by just family and a few friends. The pilot stayed away, but was seen at the graveside a few days later. After the funeral Luke and his father just carried on their daily lives, also only talking about daily practical matters. He never mentioned her to Luke, and if Luke asked any questions he would divert the conversation onto some other subject. He put away all the photographs, including their wedding photographs, and mementos he had of her in a drawer. Within a month the pilot himself died as a result of the horrific burns he sustained in the crash. The love those two people had for each other was buried with them in separate graves.

******

Luke had begun to have some difficulty in getting to sleep. One night, however, he had a vivid dream. He dreamt he was in bed, and that lying on top of him was a leopard. In the dream he was scared of moving as the leopard might attack him. But he wanted to move because he was uncomfortable as the leopard was very heavy. So he moved very carefully so as not to disturb the leopard, yet this was in vain as when he moved the leopard stirred. Then, still in the dream, Luke decided to get out of bed. He went downstairs to the kitchen with the leopard following him. In the kitchen he opened the fridge and took out some sausages. He then opened the back door and threw the sausages outside into the garden. The leopard went outside and ate the sausages, looking at Luke as he did so. He no longer felt afraid of the leopard, and he no longer felt him to be a burden. Luke then woke up.

He sat up in his bed, recounting the dream. Why did he have this dream? What did it mean? Was it telling him something? Did the leopard signify something? He got out of bed, by now wide awake. Putting on his coat and shoes he went downstairs, out of the back door and walked in the moonlight onto the common, to the place where the plane had crashed. He was in the same place he had been when the pilot had run towards him on fire. Now it was all quiet. He sat down on the ground, keeping very still. He could hear a fox barking. He thought about the pilot, and how it had seemed he was trying to tell him something. He thought about the pen and how it may contain some sort of message, or a series of messages, or maybe it was leading him in a certain direction. He thought about the leopard, which in his dream was at first a burden and a worry but then much less so. He thought about the common and how their efforts to protect or save it had got nowhere, and how he couldn't see a way forward, a way through all the difficulties. As he sat there he resolved to himself that he had to find a way, the way, and he must never, ever give up, as his aunt had told him. He did not know yet what the way was, how difficult the path ahead was, but what he found that night as he walked back home was a new determination to do all he could to save the common. He knew that in the past he had been too accepting of how things were without questioning how things could be different, and, more importantly, how he could make things

112

different. He had found a new strength within himself. He was no longer a victim.

******

Poland. Alina had been staying with her aunt, uncle and cousins in the Polish countryside for a few weeks. She was struck by the warmth she had received from all the members of her family, and was surprised how relaxed she felt in their company, and how she could speak her mother tongue not only at home but when out and about in the local community. She also loved trying to teach English to her cousins, laughing at the way they struggled to get their pronunciations correct. She told them all about her life in England, and about living next to the common, and promised her cousins that she would keep in touch and that they would always be welcome to come and stay with her and her parents, but only when they had been able to move out of their hut in the camp and into a proper house.

She knew, however, that her stay there was time-limited, and that soon she would have to leave. Having made an issue with her parents about not wanting to go to Poland, she now found at least part of herself not wishing to leave Poland. But leave she must, and there were plenty of hugs, kisses and tears when it was time to go. Although she was going to miss them all she also looked forward to being back at home again with her parents, as well as seeing Luke again. She had no idea what had befallen the common whilst she had been away.

7.

A Letter

Summer had arrived, and the birds were well into making their voices heard again. But this was not the case on the common. The ploughed up areas of the common were producing crops of potatoes which were now ready for harvesting. Luke still minded his cattle and just about found enough of the common that had not been ploughed for them to feed on. He and the cattle watched the tractor going up and down on what had been a particularly good area for grazing. He still could not believe what his own eyes were telling him, and far less accept it.

At home in the evening Luke would sit in his bedroom and sometimes hold the fountain pen that had belonged to the pilot killed in the fire. Turning it in his fingers he felt a strong connection with the pilot, someone he never knew. He now knew that his mother and the pilot were lovers, and, rather than disturb him in some way, this knowledge made him feel a kind of friendliness towards him, as he sensed that the pilot had made his mother so very happy. He understood that his mother had absolutely no regrets about what had happened, and so he didn't have any regrets either. He told himself that he was meant to find the pen, and that it still had something more to tell him, but he did not know what that was. It had become a precious item for him, more precious than a jewel or a lucky charm, something like a key without a lock. Luke knew he had to find the lock and turn the key.

He decided it was time to find out if the people he had talked to had been able to find out anything useful that might save the common. He came up with a plan, and at breakfast he told his father what he had in mind.

"Why don't we invite the people who are keen to save the common round here so that we can see if there is anything we can all do?"

His father did not answer straight away, but then said: "We haven't had any visitors like that here in years, not since your mother died. I'm not sure it's right....it's not really set up to have a lot of people round....but if it's what you want I suppose we could do it. It'll be up to you to invite people round and make everyone comfortable around the table here in the kitchen. This Saturday evening would be OK I suppose"

"Thanks Dad, thanks." With that he was off on his bicycle, firstly to look after the cattle and then to tell people that they were invited round for a get-together on Saturday evening.

The first person to arrive was the Flight Commander Porter. He shook Luke and his father by the hand and Luke showed him to the best chair in the kitchen, the only one that was not in need of some repair. Silence. The others followed soon afterwards. Harriet Crumble the butterfly lady, Luke's aunt Jean Williams, Mrs Thompson, Bill Westwood the commoner and finally Sir Geoffrey. They were left to find somewhere to sit. Miss Crumble sat perched rather unsteadily on a stool, Mrs Williams sat on a broken chair that only had three legs so he had to position herself rather carefully. Mr Westwood sat on two upturned milk crates, one on top of the other, and Mrs Thompson sat on the fridge. Sir Geoffrey chose to stand, leaning on his stick. Luke sat on another chair and his father put the kettle on and made them each of them a mug of tea, placing a packet of sugar on the table along with a teaspoon. He opened a cupboard and took out a packet of Custard Cream biscuits and another of shortbread fingers, and spread them out on a plate on the table.

"Help yourselves. We don't stand on ceremony here" and he then went and sat on top of the cupboard, away from the group who were all sat around the table.

When everyone had helped themselves to the refreshments on offer, in varying degrees of comfort, Luke spoke up.

"Thanks everyone for coming. I just wanted to hear if people had any more thoughts following on from the public meeting and what has happened since then to see if there is anything we can do to save the common."

Flight Commander Porter was the first to speak. "I did contact the Ministry of Defence and the RAF about the need for some sort of memorial on the common in memory of the servicemen who lost their lives here in protecting our country but they weren't that interested. They sent round some chappie who went on about how they get many requests of this sort, and that he was very busy, and then he left. He had added that the common was no longer needed as an airfield, and that it was up to the owners to do whatever they wanted to do. People died here in the service of their country. The spot where the plane crashed which caused the death of one of our best pilots, as Luke well knows, is now a potato field. The memories are being lost. I've also spoken to our local Member of Parliament, a young chappie, very pleasant, about it, but he told me we should be looking forwards now, not backwards. So I'm afraid I've drawn a bit of a blank."

"I'm not surprised" said Bill Westwood. "Right bunch of charlies the lot of them. That new MP isn't from round here, he's been bussed up from London way, so what does he know about the common, what does he understand about all that has gone on here and the need to preserve the memories? Piss all, pardon my French."

Harriet Crumble was the next to speak, composing herself and making sure she was sat safely on her stool first. "As you all know, I am here representing the rare blue butterfly. The butterfly doesn't have any votes, any money, any power at all. For those reasons it has been wiped out throughout this region, and now the common is the only place, the only place, within over fifty miles of here where it still survives. And it is not going to be here much longer if all this ploughing is allowed to continue to take up more and more of the common. So what can be done to save it, that's the question. Who or what organisation can do anything about it? Is there any way to protect such a vulnerable, beautiful creature? I can lie down in front of a tractor all day long but that is not going to save it in the long term, is it? The butterfly has no protection in law, as far as I am aware, and there's nobody I know of who can do anything to help it as far as I can see. Don't get me wrong, I am desperately keen to see it saved, and I'm not getting any younger, but I don't have the answer as to how to save it. But I do have the support of a group of people, some of them young people, who are keen to see the butterfly saved."

"Well spoken, Miss" said Bill Westwood. "I did speak to a solicitor friend of mine in The Fox the other night who knows a lot about the law. And I asked him about the ploughing of the common and where it stands legally. He said he thought that it was up to the commoners. The problem is that as long as whoever is doing the ploughing leaves enough grazing for any of the commoners who turn out their livestock onto the common, then it may be OK by the law, although this is not certain. And at present it is only young Luke here who exercises commoners' rights by turning out his cattle. The rest of the commoners chose not to exercise their rights any more for whatever reason, so it's game, set and match to the tractors, the plough and the potatoes. He knows his stuff and, although I don't like what he told me, I can see the logic. We could go and get a second opinion, but it would cost us, and I think what I was told is probably correct, though it pains me to say it. So we could start a legal action, but it would cost an arm and a leg, with no guarantee of success whatsoever, and likely to drag on through the courts for years. Probably not the wisest course of action, to put it mildly. I rest my case, your honour."

People laughed. A pause followed, before Luke spoke again. "Thanks everyone for what they've said so far. Maybe not really what we all wanted to hear, but thanks anyway. Mrs Thompson, have you got anything to add?"

"What I'm going to say follows on from what Bill said. I did speak to Mr Biggar. You probably remember that he came to the public meeting and told us, as an agent of the owners, that the owners could do what they liked with the common as far as he was concerned. He is right to say that practically all commons are owned by someone or somebody, and that it is widely held myth that they are not owned, or that they are owned by the monarch, the government, the council or the public. They are owned by someone, and he told me that this common is owned by a company based overseas."

"Overseas!" shouted Bill Westwood. "Heaven help us."

Whereabouts?" asked Luke.

"When I went to see Mr Biggar he was able to explain to me that the title deeds were quite in order, and that there is no barrier to prevent a company based abroad from owning land here. He declined to tell me where this company was based. He went on to say that the company asked to arrange for large parts of the common to be let to local farmers so that the company would receive some rent, and that is what has happened. As far as I can make out, therefore, they are the legal owners. Why did an overseas company come to own it? Probably as some way of making some income and of avoiding paying tax. Maybe even as speculation that the value of the land would rise in the future. Mr Biggar is just carrying out their instructions, and the common will be used to grow potatoes. As a farmer myself I don't approve of poor quality, marginal land being used in this way. You can say what you like about a national food shortage, but growing crops should only be done on richer, more fertile soils, not these sandy soils in my opinion. But there we are, and that's the reality of the matter."

Bill Westwood responded. "I think that's crazy, but maybe it is the way of the world now and in the future, just plain crazy if you ask me. I'm going to have to have another biscuit", helping himself to a Custard Cream.

Sir Geoffrey cleared his throat and began to speak. "My family has known the common for many, many years, and I believe my ancestors were once the legal owners. For that reason I find what is currently happening there... difficult. Whilst I can support farmers given the need for them to produce more crops, I do think that it should not be at the expense of the common. What can be done about it? I'm afraid I just don't see a way forward."

"So, we've found out that there is nothing that can be done to save the common" said Mrs Thompson.

"I'm sorry for bringing you all here for nothing" said Luke. He paused, then continued. "If only we could just buy it, that would solve everything" he said, half jokingly.

"Indeed" said Jean Williams, who had been quiet up to this point. "That is the one solution to all of this. And you are right Luke, for this is the one solution we should work towards."

Everyone looked at Jean Williams intently. Harriet Crumble straightened her back on the stool, Bill Westwood choked on his Custard Cream, and the Flight Commander leant forward to listen, fiddling with his moustache, saying "We buy it?"

"Yes" said Luke "We buy it."

Bill Westwood spoke. "Are you out of your mind, pardon me? I'm sat here on two upturned milk crates, and you suggest we pay thousands and thousands of pounds, money we haven't got, to a company based overseas for the common".

"We have to find the money."

Luke's father was speechless. This had never occurred to him, mainly because he was not familiar with any property buying and selling, or any amounts of money beyond what he gets by way of his small wage packets. He thought surely this can't be realistic.

"Pardon me" said the Flight Commander, "But is it for sale? Do we know that?"

"It may not be for sale, but it is up to us, everyone in this room, to do what we can to persuade the owners to sell it at the right price and to raise the necessary money" replied Jean Williams. "Luke is absolutely right, it is the one solution, and sometimes you have to think ambitiously if you want to get anywhere. Otherwise we can just sit here wringing our hands and getting nowhere."

At this point there was a knock on the back door.

"I'll go" said Luke, and he left the room, shaking his head at what he had just heard and trying to make sense of it, and opened the back door. Standing outside was Alina. Luke took a sharp intake of breath and stared at her, saying nothing.

"All right, no need to look as if you've just seen a ghost, it's only me. Just thought I would call round to see what's going on." said Alina as she brushed past him.

"Alina" whispered Luke. He felt everything was spinning in his head, and, feeling an onrush of emotion, he stepped outside into the fresh evening air. He was already trying to digest the idea of purchasing the common and now he had the shock of seeing Alina again to deal with as well. "Alina's back" he whispered again. He could feel his breath quickening and he took some deep breaths before going back inside to join the others.

People were now beginning to talk through what Luke's aunt had suggested. Alina was standing in a corner listening to what was being said. Luke went and stood next to his father. His auntie Jean was speaking.

"There is no other option if we are serious about saving the common. We have to get organised, negotiate with the owners, start raising the funds, gain the support of the wider public, get them to open their purses and get campaigning. There is no other way."

Another long silence.

"What you mean is that we have to form a committee, open a bank account, register ourselves as a charitable trust, get properly organised, start negotiating with the owners through their agent and start campaigning if we are to save the common" said the Flight Commander.

"That's it in a nutshell" replied Jean Williams. "Sounds quite straightforward said like that, but it will be a huge effort. Can we succeed? I know we can. Why? Because right is on our side. Ploughing up the common may or may not be illegal as the law stands, just as depriving the butterfly of a home and making it go extinct may not be illegal, but that does not mean to say it is right, because it isn't. I believe we have right on our side and saving the common will strike a chord with many people and organisations out there, many of whom would be willing to dig into their pockets. And some of them have big pockets. Using the common to grow potatoes takes away not only the grazing land of the commoners but also the butterfly, the wildflowers, the birds, the pleasure of going for a countryside walk in a large open space. And it gives us farmers a bad name. I'd be happy to take the reins as Chair of the committee. So, who's going to help?"

Harriet Crumble spoke up. "It feels I've been waiting a long, long time to hear someone speak up like that. I have been so angry about what has been happening to the common, but now is the chance to turn all that angry protest into some positive action. At last I can see some light ahead for the beautiful butterfly and its home here on the common. Thank you, thank you Mrs Williams. I will give you every possible support. My partner Joan is good with figures and I'm sure she would be happy to do the accounts."

Luke's father was next. "I don't get involved much with things in the community, I've kept myself to myself for many years, but I suppose it is time now to stand up and be counted. I don't know what I can do to help, but my son Luke here will be willing to help in any way he can, and he has my blessing. As for me, I can stand in the town and rattle a tin to gain a few pennies for the cause."

"I think this is an excellent idea" said the Flight Commander. "What can I do to help? I have contacts that may be of use, and I'm used to meetings and could be Secretary for the Committee."

Bill Westwood was the last to speak. "We could make a challenge in the courts against the ploughing, despite what my friend said. But then we could end up losing the case and having to pay thousands of pounds in lawyers' fees. What's the sense in that? To start down a road that more likely than not would finish up with the lawyers getting richer whilst we get a lot poorer makes no sense. So why not buy the land? They're not making any more land, so it would be a sound investment, and of course it would give us control over what happens on the common, stopping the ploughing on day one I suggest. So I'm all in favour, as long as we can get the money together, and it will mean getting a huge amount of money together."

Jean Williams spoke again. "It seems we are all agreed then, to set up a committee with a view to purchasing the common. I suppose we'd better have a vote on it. All in favour raise your hands." All hands were raised. "It will be far from easy, but I think we can do it. We need a couple of figureheads to lead the campaign. I suggest Luke is one, as he has been the instigator of getting us together, and this is all about the future of the common, and as a young person he embodies the future. And this is about the future, about a new chapter for the common. Are you up for it Luke?"

"You bet. I'll do anything to save the common" replied Luke. Alina smiled at the new note of confidence in his voice.

"We also need something as well as someone to represent the common, a symbol if you like. It could be the skylark, but perhaps it should be the blue butterfly. What do you think Miss Crumble?"

Harriet Crumble replied without any hestitation. "Unless we all work as hard as we can the butterfly will disappear, as it has from so many sites round here. This is its last stand, and it has a special status here. I will promote it, shout about it, talk about it, show it to people, write about it, campaign about it, rattle tins in the street for it and do anything I can to save it. It will make a marvellous emblem for the campaign, and it will make me feel very proud that you should think of it as such. I may be called Crumble, but crumble I will not! I....NEVER.... CRUMBLE! And by the way, you can call me Harriet if you like."

"Thank you Harriet" replied Jean Williams. "Well, I think that's about it for this evening. Let's meet again next week to start some more detailed planning."

"Just one thing though" said Bill Westwood as people were getting to their feet. "If we're going to buy it we really do need to know who we are buying it from and where they are based, what their address is. We can't just go through Mr Biggar, we need to be in contact with the owners direct it seems to me. We need to contact the organ grinder and not just rely on the monkey. So I suggest that me and Luke here have another go at Mr Biggar to get the information from him by calling round at his offices. What do you think?"

There was a general murmuring of agreement, with Luke adding that he was more than willing to go.

Alina spoke. "I would like to come as well," and Luke smiled.

The meeting broke up, with everyone standing up and shaking hands, and following Harriet Crumble's lead, introducing themselves to each other on first name terms.

A few days later Luke and Alina met with Bill Westwood and they travelled the twenty miles to Mr Biggar's office by train. On the train Luke and Alina were able to talk.

"When I got back my parents told me about the ploughing on the common. I went to see it for myself, and I was disgusted. So I came round to see you. I had no idea there was a meeting going on."

"We're going to save the common" said Luke. "We're going to do more than that, we're going to buy it." He was still on excited by the outcome of the meeting.

"I can see you've changed, not quite the same timid lad I used to know."

"How was Poland?"

"It was good to see other members of my family again. But in truth it all felt a bit strange. I know I am Polish, but I have spent so many years here that this feels as much like home as Poland does. Couldn't see myself living back there. But I am still Polish, I speak Polish with my parents, we eat Polish food and celebrate Polish culture. It's all a bit mixed up. I was glad to get back here."

On arrival at the offices they were met by a receptionist, who asked them to wait as Mr Biggar was busy with a phone call. A few minutes later Mr Biggar emerged from his office and shook all three of them by the hand.

"Rather than go into my office let's go into the meeting room and discuss matters there" he said, ushering them into a large room next to his office with a long table and six chairs placed neatly along each side. There was wood panelling on the walls and prints of countryside and hunting scenes. Against one wall a bookcase stood with rows of identical volumes of legal proceedings and case law. The chairs were upholstered in leather and the table was made of oak and polished to shine like a mirror.

"Please sit where you like." The three of them sat on one side, and Mr Biggar sat across the table from them. The atmosphere was tense, and Luke felt quite uncomfortable. The fact that Bill Westwood was in a setting he was so unused to, however, did not seem to bother him in the slightest.

"Now look, we won't keep you long, we just want to know who owns the common."

"I can't tell you that."

"Why the bloody hell not?"

"It's confidential, that's why."

"Why is it confidential?"

"Because the people who own it have asked me to keep it confidential."

"Why don't you tell us who it is and then we can ask them why they want to keep it confidential?"

"Because it's confidential."

"You see we know you're just the middleman here, and it's nothing to you really, so why not just tell us – we won't let anyone know who told us. Here, you can write it down on a piece of paper rather than say it if that would help" as he took out a scrumpled up piece of paper, and a pencil from behind his ear.

"You're not going to get it out of me, I'm afraid" replied Mr Biggar.

At this point Alina spoke up. "Excuse me, but could I use your toilet please?"

"Second door on the right, young lady" replied Mr Biggar.

Alina left the meeting, and as she walked out she saw that the first door on the right had Mr Biggar's name on it, and that the door was slightly ajar. She saw that the receptionist had her back to her. She went into the office and looked around. Lots of papers on the desk, and lots of box files in the bookcase behind the desk. Each file had a name written on the outside, and they were all lined up alphabetically. She looked at them, scanning all the names, until she spotted one entitled Heathland Holdings. It was high up, so she pulled up a chair and stood on it. She stretched her arm, but the file was still too high. So she stood on one of the arms of the chair and stretched again. The chair tilted. Her mind went back to when she stood on the milk crate outside the parish hall to hear what was being said there. She knew if she fell they would be a big crash and she would be found out, so she relaxed for a moment, before tilting the chair again so it stood on just two of its legs. The chair wobbled. Alina stretched a bit further. Her fingers managed to get on top of the file and she pulled it out. The file came off the shelf and started to fall towards the floor, but Alina managed to catch it just in time. She paused, motionless, for a few seconds, hoping that the sound of her catching the file had not been picked up by anyone else. She sat down on the chair and quickly opened the file and looked at the contents. She recognised lots of maps of the common. There was plenty of letters as well, which had addresses on. Alina took out one from near the top addressed to Mr Biggar, folded it roughly and put it down the front of her blouse. She managed to replace the file and the chair, then she looked out of the door and saw that the receptionist still had her back turned towards her and was speaking on the phone whilst filing her nails. She left the office, went into the toilet, paused for a minute, flushed the toilet, and made her way back to the meeting room.

The meeting was on the point of breaking up, as everyone was getting to their feet. More hand shaking, and they left the building.

"Well that got us precisely absolutely no bloody where whatsoever" said Bill Westwood as they walked along the street and arrived at the station. The train duly arrived, and they took their seats.

"I've got this" said Alina as she pulled out a piece of paper from under her blouse.

"What's that" asked Luke.

"It's a letter addressed to Mr Biggar. I took it from his office."

"You did what?" shouted Luke, but Mr Westwood grinned, saying "Good on you girl. That's a fair girlfriend you've got there Luke, she knows what to do all right, and she's got some guts." With that he took out his tobacco tin and cigarette papers, rolled a thin cigarette and lit it, drawing heavily on it.

"Well, what does it say?" asked Luke.

"Is there an address? asked Bill Westwood.

Alina looked at the top of the letter. "It says 'Heathland Holdings, PO Box 6385, Bermuda. Where's Bermuda?" asked Alina.

"Somewhere far, far away, in the Caribbean Sea….or maybe in the Atlantic Ocean for all I know. A British Government territory and a well-known tax haven" replied Bill Westwood. "At least we've learnt something today, maybe not from Mr Biggar. Christ, are we up against it, and the people who are in control of all of this, pulling all the levers, are thousands of miles away. How on earth are we going to have any influence on them."

Luke and Alina looked glum, before Alina spoke again.

"Luke, you read out what the letter says."

Luke took the letter. "It says: Dear Mr Biggar, Thank you for keeping us informed about developments on the common. We were glad to hear that the ploughing and planting of the potatoes has gone well with the minimum of interference from the local busybodies…"

"That'll be the likes of us" interrupted Mr Westwood proudly, with a glint in his eye.

"…including that eccentric butterfly woman, and that the tenant farmer has got on with the necessary work. We look forward to receiving the rent money we are due from him in due course.

"You will be aware, however, that this is only the first step regarding our plans for the common. As you will know, the common sits on vast reserves of sand and gravel, and these will need to be exploited, especially as the demand for more housing locally increases. Destroying the heathland by ploughing and growing crops was just the first stage. Soon we will be serving notice on the tenant farmer, whatever his name is. He may have done a reasonable job but he is surplus to what we want to happen eventually. We will be contacting you again in the near future to discuss how we can best put this long term plan into effect, probably asking you to arrange some test excavations in the first instance. Yours sincerely...' I can't read the signature, but underneath it says Heathland Holdings."

Bill Westwood spoke again, this time more sombrely and more slowly than before. "We've got ploughing destroying our grazing land, and next will come massive earth diggers removing sand and gravel if they have their way. So they are not content just to destroy the common, they want to physically remove it in lorries and take it somewhere else, basically as part of hundreds of buildings. Lorry load after lorry load will be taken off the common. Good to hear that Mr Hughes will get his comeuppance, but not at the expense of seeing the common wiped out. What would be left after they take all the sand and gravels? Just some gravel pits filled with water. Heathland Holdings....more like Heathland Hooligans if you ask me."

Luke and Alina said nothing for a while. The atmosphere became colder, quickly replacing the sense of achievement they had experienced in finding out who owned the common, as the implications of the letter dawned on them. They both looked out of the train window as they tried to piece together their thoughts.

"Can we stop this?" said Luke. "At least we now know what the plans are, unlike when they started all the ploughing, which just came as a complete shock to all of us. So this time we can form a plan of our own I suppose."

"Well said Luke. That's what we need, a plan to defeat their plan. And all thanks to your girlfriend here."

Alina paused for a moment, glanced at Luke, but decided not to issue her customary denial of any romantic association with Luke this time. Instead she said "All I did was stand on a chair and reach up for a file I thought may relate to the common and remove the letter on top of all the other papers. Mind you, I very nearly fell off, and that would have given me away."

"Good job you didn't or we would all have been shown the door smartish. A bit of undercover detective work, a bit of bending the rules here and there, some going where you're not meant to go, all these can have benefits at times. And if we are found out we just have to take any punishment we are due. Will Mr Biggar miss the letter and think that we stole it, or will he think that he must have just put it somewhere other than in the file and lost it? Who knows? Who cares?" said Bill Westwood.

"But the key thing is now we know who they are, where they are and what they want" said Luke, and he continued in a serious tone. "And that gives us the opportunity we need. All the way along so far we have been kept in the dark, and in a way the darkness just got deeper, but now we can begin to shine some light."

One evening when Luke and his father were at home there was a knock at the door and auntie Jean entered.

"I thought I would call round to see how you are both getting on" she said.

Luke put down the tea towel he had been using to dry the dishes, and his father dried his hands on another towel as they both sat down at the table.

"Not too bad, thank you. And thanks for coming. We don't get many visitors, although that has changed a bit since all this activity started on the common. What can we do for you?"

"I wanted firstly to hear from Luke how things are for him, as it's a while ago since I told him about his mother and the pilot."

"Better said Luke. "Much better. I feel I understand things more, and I feel more….confident, better able to speak up for myself."

"I know you're use to helping people through the work you do looking after children, and it has certainly paid dividends with Luke. He's a much happier boy, or young man, now than before. Why don't you sit yourself down?" added his father.

"And how about you, Peter? said Jean looking at Luke's father.

"What do you mean? I'm just my normal self, carrying on with the daily grind I suppose."

"Dad, auntie Jean and I talked about Mum, what had happened between her and the pilot, about her dying, about things you and I have never talked about before. Don't you think the time has come to talk about what happened rather than carrying it around like a huge weight pressing down on you all the time? We're never going to be able to look to the future with any belief if you remain so bound up in the past and what took place then."

"She was a fine woman, your mother, as I've always said. Of course I knew about her and the pilot, or rather I guessed what was going on. Nothing I could do about it. It hurt, of course it hurt, and still does if I stop to think about it, and that's why I try not to think about it. That's why there are no photographs, no mementoes of her in the house. It's not that I didn't love her, of course I did, it's just that it's all too painful. I could well understand that eventually she was probably going to find someone better than me, someone more educated perhaps, someone who shared her interests more. Things may have been very different if they both hadn't died, but all that about the pilot was nothing to do with me, despite what others may have said. All I did at the time was to try and protect you from all of it, by not talking about it. It was all so difficult at the time. So few people wanted to have anything to do with me, and I just shut myself away anyway. The only ones who visited me and showed some kindness were the Polish family, Alina's family. The others just didn't want to know, or kept making snide comments under their breath. I knew what they were thinking - a jealous man, a cuckold, one of the stuck-in-the-past commoners, maybe even a murderer. Maybe I was wrong not to confront all these things at the time, I don't know. It was a very hard time, and I just felt that we, or rather I, should just keep our heads down and battle through it."

"You were wrong, Peter, although I can understand why you bottled it all up" said Jean. "It all happened several years ago now, but if you don't go through the pain of grief you get stuck in anger and helplessness. Perhaps Luke has dealt with it better that you, by asking questions and finding answers. The two of you need to spend time together to talk openly about her. Visiting her grave together and laying some flowers on it – she so loved flowers – would be a good place to start. How about it?"

Luke's father spoke first. "All these years and I've never had the courage to visit her grave. It's been like a brick wall that I couldn't get through. I know how hard I would find it, but I will go, with you Luke, together we will go. Maybe the grave will need some attention as well, it may be overgrown with weeds for all I know, and we will make sure it is properly cared for."

Then Luke spoke. "It does need some attention, as I saw it recently and it is getting overgrown. The headstone needs cleaning. We can take a trowel and a fork as well as some flowers, and maybe something to plant as well. It would be good to do this together, on a nice day. And we can take the photographs out of the drawer and put them on the dresser. It would be like letting her back into our lives."

Auntie Jean went to get her coat and left the two of them alone.

Luke was on the common again. It was pouring with rain and his cattle had gone inside the old RAF control tower to shelter. Much of the common was now bare earth, as the potatoes had been harvested. He saw Mr Hughes walking across the common.

At that point Luke heard the rumbling of a machine, but as he looked up this time he didn't see a tractor but rather a large digger. The digger drove across the common. Luke knew why the digger was there, and he also guessed that Mr Hughes didn't know why the digger was there. He saw Mr Hughes walk across to the digger, and, thinking he would love to know the sort of conversation that was going to take place, he walked over there as well. When he arrived the digger had dug a huge hole three feet deep. Another man was present and he jumped into the hole and collected a sample of the sand and gravels with a spade and put them into a large sack. The man with the spade measured the depth of the hole and then told the driver of the digger to dig deeper.

"Excuse me" said Mr Hughes "but may I ask you what on earth you are doing. I have a tenancy on this land to farm it to produce crops."

The man with the spade stopped what he was doing, climbed out of the hole the digger had made and looked at Mr Hughes. "We're here to measure the extent and amount of sand and gravel that is available for extraction across the whole common. Now, if you don't mind…"

"You're here to do what?" bellowed Mr Hughes. "I suggest you take that machine of yours off here immediately. You've no business to do any such thing."

"We are instructed by the agent, Mr Biggar, who acts for the owners of the common. If you have any problem with what we are doing I respectfully suggest you contact him. Now, really, we have work to do here."

"Mr Biggar hasn't told me anything about this."

"Then you need to contact him."

"But what about my crops? What about my tenancy agreement? It may have only been an annual agreement, but I was given to believe that it would last more than a couple of years."

"Again, you need to speak to Mr Biggar. If you don't mind, we shall need to take some samples from your potato fields next."

"And what if I do mind?"

"You can speak to Mr Biggar."

"You can speak to Mr Biggar, you can speak to Mr Biggar. Are you some kind of robot?"

Luke stood there not fully knowing what to make of it. He obviously despised Mr Hughes for having ploughed up part of the common, and he obviously despised the digger driver and the man with the spade for threatening to extract all the sand and gravel from the common. Who was worse? Or was it just a case of a plague on both your houses? Part of him found the whole situation a strange comedy, and yet part knew that both were intent on wrecking the common, his heritage.

"And you can take that grin off your face" said Mr Hughes, staring at Luke. Luke found himself unable to take the grin off his face, and he just shook his head whilst he enjoyed seeing Mr Hughes going redder and redder in the face.

"Hit a snag have we, Mr Hughes?" he said, feeling emboldened by what was taking place. Mr Hughes averted his gaze, and walked away briskly without saying anything else. Luke then looked at the man with the spade. He felt an increasing sense of confidence, but he also knew that the threat posed by the digger and the man with the spade was much greater than that posed by Mr Hughes.

"If you think for one moment that I and others are going to accept your plans to dig up all the sands from here you are very much mistaken."

"Young man, we are just exploring the options at present, nothing more than that."

At this moment Luke heard someone approaching from behind. He turned round and saw Mr Westwood walking towards him, stick in hand and rolled-up cigarette stuck to his bottom lip.

"I saw the digger come on to the common. Exploring options, you liar. We know your game, and it's to take the common from the likes of us."

"I'm afraid we haven't been introduced" responded the man with the spade.

"I'm not afraid, but I'm not bloody well delighted either. Bill Westwood's my name and I lived here by the common all my life. I don't need to know your name, it's what you're up to that's more important. Now it's a waste of your time and mine if you just stand there going on about options. You are determined to dig out all the sand that has been here since the last ice age, put it in trucks and take it away some place else. That is a devastation of the common. The chap you just said goodbye to was bad enough with his ploughing and potatoes, but you are ten times worse."

"I'm just doing my job, as instructed by the agent for the owners. If you're not happy you need to speak to Mr Biggar."

"And what permission have you got for this? Do the local council know about it?"

"You will need to speak to Mr Biggar."

"Come on young Luke, waste of time standing here and getting no answers" kicking some sand back into the pit that had been excavated by the digger.

They left the digger driver and the man with the spade to carry on taking samples. As they walked off the common Mr Westwood turned to Luke and said "Now this I do know. They will need the permission of the local council if they want to dig out all that sand. And will they have a fight on their hands? You bet. We will have to get ourselves organised. The owners will be throwing a lot of money at this. Maybe we can even get Mr Hughes on our side." They both smiled, despite the fact that by this time the persistent rain had soaked them completely.

"Young Luke, I can see you've got a real taste for a fight. And it will be a real fight, believe me."

An application for extraction of the sand and gravel was duly submitted to the local council. Members of the group, now called Save Our Common, went round the neighbourhood asking people to sign a petition opposing the application, and within a few weeks over five hundred people had signed. The petition was sent to the chairperson of the council planning committee to demonstrate the strength of feeling in the area about the application, and that it wasn't just a small group of interested people who were opposing it.

No more work was done on the common with the digger, and Mr Hughes was allowed to continue with his cultivations. The group wondered if they should approach Mr and Mrs Hughes to see if they would sign the petition, and a letter was sent asking him if he would like to sign it, but, as they expected, no reply was received. Another person who was approached was the rector, and Luke decided to go and visit him in person.

When he arrived at the rectory Luke knocked on the door and the rector opened it and started speaking at him before he had the chance to cross the threshold. He continued talking as he led Luke into his dining room where he sat on a chair and gestured to Luke to sit on a chair next to him.

"Ah, yes. I suppose you are going to ask me to sign the petition I have heard so much about from members of my congregation, who all seem to have signed it and have encouraged me to do likewise. Well, I suppose so….and maybe I was wrong all the way along….sometimes we all make mistakes….I didn't understand how vital the common was to so many people….I just saw what people termed progress as a good thing….some members of the congregation have felt so strongly about it that there has been a suggestion that perhaps I should step down…. my curate has advised me to change my stance….it's not something I generally do, but I have given it a lot of thought, and indeed prayer….and….well, as I said, we all make mistakes at times, and I have to admit that….well, I suppose I have to ask for your forgiveness. Give me the petition and I will sign it now."

To say that Luke was taken aback would be an understatement, and yet in a way he was not completely surprised. He knew that right was on his side, and that the rector had come to realise that he had been in the wrong.

"And there were those comments, or suggestions, you made about my mother. There's no need for me to forgive you. The important thing is that you have come to understand that the common should be left alone, and valued as it is, and I now understand that, despite what you and others may have said or felt, my mother did nothing wrong. She just fell in love with someone, that's all, and it can happen to any of us at any time."

The rector was clearly embarrassed. He fumbled in his pockets for a pen, and as he was about to get up to go and find one, Luke produced the pilot's pen.

"Here, use this."

"Thank you. How did you get to own a quality pen like that?"

"I found it." Luke chose not to divulge anything more about the pen, and the irony of getting the rector to sign the petition with the pilot's pen was not lost on him. As the rector signed the petition Luke came to realise again the power of the pen, the pen that once belonged to his mother's lover, and that his mother may once have touched. A pen that had started him on a path to protect his heritage. He thanked the rector, smiled at him, gave him a wink and left.

By now it was winter. The campaign group decided that as many people as possible should go to the council committee meeting when the application was due to be heard and determined, so more posters went up locally inviting people to come along. Despite the cold weather around forty people lined the steps of the council building on the day of the council committee meeting convened to decide the fate of the common. All the people Luke knew were there, as well as many other local people. Some carried placards and banners. One just said HANDS OFF OUR COMMON, another, held by Miss Crumble, said SAVE THE BLUE BUTTERFLY. Bill Westwood had made a placard out of a piece of old cardboard and a length of wood, with just two words written in capital letters in black paint – BIGGAR OFF. He was in a jovial mood, as were all of the group, who saw it as a celebration of what the common meant to each of them. Even Sir Geoffrey was there, smartly dressed in a tweed suit.

A council employee came outside to greet the protestors, and asked to speak to their spokesperson. Luke was ushered forward, partly by Alina who was there with her parents but also by other members of the group, including his father.

"Now we just about have space for all of you to attend the meeting, although some of you will have to sit on the floor. But we can't allow all of you to speak. The applicant, Mr Biggar (loud booing ensued) will be given ten minutes to put forward his case, and then one person from your group will have the floor for ten minutes. I will be timing each, and as soon as the ten minutes are up I will ask each to stop talking. Everyone who attends the meeting will have to behave themselves or else they will be escorted out. So, are you the one from your group who is going to speak on its behalf to oppose the application, or will it be someone else?"

Luke looked round. This was all unfamiliar territory for him, and he supposed for everyone in the group. His father was stood by his side, and he asked everyone to gather round and listen for a moment.

"We have to have just one spokesperson to address the meeting. Any suggestions anybody?"

"It should be Luke" said one voice, and quickly everyone else agreed, with no other name put forward.

"So, young man" continued the council employee "You've heard the rules about addressing the meeting. Do you have any questions?"

Luke stood there unable to think of any questions as his mind was too full of thinking what he would have to say, and his heart was a mixture of pride in representing the common and the group, excitement at never having had to address such a meeting before and fear that he might get it all wrong. He was too busy trying to process all the points he needed to get across to think of any questions.

"Good" said the council employee, "I'll call you in when we are ready to make a start."

They didn't have to wait long before being called into the council chamber. The chairperson was seated at a table with the other councillors also at tables on either side forming a horseshoe shape. The protestors sat at the far end, some on chairs and some on the floor. The chairperson called the meeting to order. She glanced at the protestors, spotted Bill Westwood's placard and said in a no-nonsense voice, "Would all members of the group before me please put down their placards, thank you." Bill Westwood and the others did as they were told.

She continued. "We are here to decide on the application to extract sand and gravels from the common. Mr Biggar I believe you are representing the applicant, you have ten minutes to present your case."

Mr Biggar rose to his feet, thanking the chairperson. He outlined what the application was about, how thousands of tons of sand and gravel were waiting to be exploited, and how beneficial this would be to provide the raw materials required for house building, quoting figures regarding the expanding human population in the area. He went on to say that the work would be done as sensitively as possibly to minimise the effect on the local neighbourhood. The work was scheduled to last for up to twelve years, providing jobs for local people, after which the site would be vacated. Large pools would be formed which would be excellent for wildlife such as waterfowl and amphibians, and a bird hide would be installed. The common would be a different place, but still open to the public, he said. His speech was on one occasion interrupted by some of the protestors, who cried "Shame" when he talked about the lorries taking away the sand, and the chairperson intervened with a threat of eviction for anyone who disrupted the meeting.

After a couple of questions from the councillors it was Luke's turn to speak. He rose to his feet and nervously asked for a glass of water, which was passed to him. He felt in his chest pocket for the pilot's pen, which he had brought with him to bring him luck. It was there, and he twisted it round in his fingers. He began by saying who he was and that his family had enjoyed commoners' rights over several generations, and that he tended a few cattle on the common to this day, but only on land that was left available following the ploughing. It was part of his heritage, part of who he was. He went on to say how much the common was enjoyed by so many people in so many different ways. At this point Luke stumbled. Miss Crumble, who was sitting near Luke, hastily scribbled down something on a piece of paper and passed it to Luke, who read the words it contained: The butterfly is rare. "That's right, there's a little blue butterfly on the common that can be found nowhere else for miles around. It's very beautiful, very fragile and it won't survive all the works that are being planned." This seemed to spur him on. He went on to refer to the old wartime airfield, how many people lost their lived there, how the skylarks still sang over the common in the springtime, how many families loved to come onto the common to enjoy picnics, how people loved to walk their dogs or ride their horses on the common, how special it is for rare plants that grow there. All that, he said, would be lost, as the common would be changed beyond recognition from what it has been for centuries. There are already ponds on the common. It may become something different when all the sands had been taken away, but it would not be the same. For what? So that some people who live far away from here can earn a lot of money, for the building of some houses? Luke was well into his stride by now, and he finished with a call to arms to the assembled councillors, telling them that they now had it in their power to preserve the common from its total destruction. The group of protestors broke into spontaneous applause, and the chairperson had to wield her gavel to bring the meeting to order.

As Luke sat down one of the councillors asked him a question. "If this application is rejected wouldn't you expect the ploughing and the growing of crops to continue, so that at the end of the day the common will not be saved no matter what is decided today?"

Luke knew he was expected to answer this point, and fortunately he had anticipated being asked this. He stood up again.

"We, the group of people who are assembled here today, are determined to save the common by whatever means. And even if the ploughing were to be set to continue we would be doing whatever it takes to have it stopped and the common returned to how it was and how it has been for centuries,"

"Can you please be a bit more specific as to what means you have in mind? I hope we are not talking about anything outside the law here" responded the councillor, looking over his half-moon spectacles enquiringly at Luke.

Luke hesitated, and looked behind him at the other members of the group for some inspiration or guidance as to how best to answer the question. Alina went over to him and whispered in his ear. "You have to be straight with them, be truthful. You have to tell them that we may try to buy it."

Luke composed himself, before apologising for the short delay in answering the question. The chairperson accepted his apology.

"We will not do anything outside of the law. If it were possible, and if it were the only solution to saving the common, we would like to try to purchase it from the current owners."

The councillor who asked the question looked at Mr Biggar, and asked him if he had anything to say about this.

"As far as I am aware the common is not up for sale" said Mr Biggar.

"Thank you" replied the councillor.

"But, if this application were to be rejected, surely the owners would be open to offers" said Luke hurriedly, aware that a potential weakness had been uncovered in the group's case.

"And that's all quite 'iffy' if I may use that word, quite hypothetical" said the councillor.

"All I can say is that we would do whatever we can, we are determined that the common can and should be saved and all the ploughing should be stopped and this application should be rejected" persisted Luke, to sounds of support from the group behind him.

Nobody spoke for a while, before the chairperson thanked Mr Biggar and Luke for their presentations and asked the councillors to state whether or not they supported the application and their reasons. The first to speak was the councillor who had asked Luke the questions.

"I find it very difficult to weigh the arguments, and for that reason I am minded to abstain. But this is such an important issue that it is no time to sit on the fence. Matters are less than certain as to what might happen to the common if the application were to be rejected. However, the application, if successful, would have such a serious impact on the common that I believe it should be rejected."

Cheers went up from the group, with the chairperson having to use her gavel again and call for order.

There were four other councillors present. The next one spoke.

"I have to declare an interest here. Like many people, I love to walk on the common, sometimes with our dog but more often these days without as he's getting too old now. We love the common for what it is, a beautiful, tranquil place where you can go and empty your mind of all the day-to-day worries that we all have, and breathe the fresh air. It has helped me especially when I've been feeling down, or even worse moments when you can see no point in carrying on. I don't know much about the wildlife or the blue butterfly or the rights of commoners, but I always feel better in myself after a walk on the common, and I guess that the same can be said for many other people. So I am voting to reject the application to afford the common the protection it needs."

The group remained silent this time, not daring to hope that their wish was going to come true. The atmosphere had become more tense.

Another councillor spoke. "As a business man I can see the attraction of giving much needed employment in the area by supporting this application and so creating more prosperity, which is what we all want to see. And yet….it is a case of trying to weigh the benefits of that with the costs of losing something that is quite unique. And I think in this instance the scales come down on the side of preserving the common. We have to think in the long term here, and why should something that has existed peacefully for centuries be effectively destroyed here, this afternoon. I shall be voting to reject the application."

The next councillor stood up to speak. "Some of my colleagues, madam chair, sat here today may have short memories. I do not, as I have sat on this committee for the past thirty years. Not long after I was elected, this council examined the case for a possible purchase of the common, to safeguard it for the future. In the end, it was decided not to proceed. Why? Because there were doubts and misgivings about the ownership. We weren't sure who the owners were, or, once that was established, how had they acquired the ownership. The council decided not to take the matter any further, which was a shame in my view as it would have prevented the current situation we now find ourselves in. So I fully support the stance of the Save Our Common group if they do decide to go ahead to try to purchase the common, and in fact I will ask if I may be permitted to join their group. I shall therefore be voting down this application."

Finally the last councillor spoke. "In my opinion the application is a complete affront to any notion of preserving our wonderful countryside and the creatures that live there, especially the blue butterfly. I shall wholeheartedly vote to reject it."

Amongst the group the cheers soon subsided and gave way to a feeling of incredulity as the application was rejected unanimously. As the chairperson concluded the proceedings the group burst into applause. Luke's father was the first to go up to Luke and put his arms round him, and Luke let his head sink into his father's shoulder. They had not embraced like that ever before. Luke was trying to hold back tears as he went to thank Alina for her words of advice. Bill Westwood went up to Luke and told him he had done "a right good performance.

Now's the time to get everything sorted out for good." Luke knew what he meant.

8.

The Butterfly Leads the Way

Once the planning application had been rejected the campaign group decided to move swiftly. First of all they needed a solicitor to act for them by writing a letter to the owners of the common in Bermuda. Harriet Crumble knew a local solicitor as a friend, and he agreed to write a letter free of charge on behalf of the group, whilst also making it clear that if the matter was progressed towards a purchase of the common then he would require payment. The letter asked the owners if they would be interested in selling the common to the group and, if so, could they quote a figure that would be acceptable.

A reply was received from the owners within two weeks, and the solicitor gave it to Harriet Crumble. She let members of the group know that a reply had been received and invited them to a meeting in her house.

"Well, what does it say?" said Bill Westwood impatiently everyone had arrived and sat down.

"I shall read the letter out" replied Miss Crumble.

"Dear Sirs, We refer to your recent letter asking if we would be willing to sell the common to the group your represent. We would be willing to consider an offer, but it would have to be sufficient. We are not a charity and we expect a reasonable return on our investment. So a figure based on the market value would be appropriate. We hope this is acceptable to the group and we look forward to hearing from you."

Silence as members of the group took this in. Bill Westwood spoke first.

"That means we are going to have to find an awful lot of money. They are not saying how much, but the market value means a substantial amount."

"And then there would be all the legal fees on top" added Jean Williams. "And not to mention the cost of restoring back to heathland those areas that have been ploughed up."

The group went on to discuss how they might raise money towards the purchase, and how they might agree an acceptable figure with the owners. When the meeting finished they were all conscious of the huge task facing them, but no less determined.

Various foundations and other organisations were approached, and sums of money were pledged subject to the full amount being raised. Individuals in the local area, many of whom were familiar with the common from having walked there over many years also made substantial donations, and some of them even joined the committee to make it a much larger, community-based group.

The local press was bombarded with stories and regular updates. The campaign group held a number of fund-raising events. Pride of place went to Harriet Crumble's walks and talks about the blue butterfly. She and Joan led groups of people round the parts of the common that had not been ploughed up to see the butterflies, which in the height of summer were to be seen in their hundreds, and told them about how they live in her best schoolmistress style.

"Ladies and gentlemen, boys and girls, isn't this little blue butterfly the most beautiful thing you have ever seen? So pretty, so delicate and fragile, and yet sadly so easy to get rid of. This butterfly has become rare. It wasn't rare once, but so much of the heathy places it needs have been lost, all in the name of progress. Doesn't the sight of this creature fill your heart with wonder? And once you get to know more about this particular butterfly, the more wondrous it becomes. The female butterfly lays its tiny eggs on the heather, where they stay throughout the winter. When it hatches as a tiny caterpillar in the spring it gets picked up by ants. The ants look after it and protect it from being eaten by spiders or attacked by small wasps, and in return the caterpillar gives the ants sugary liquids. That is how the world works, how everything is connected, how the plants are connected to the insects, how different creatures seek to kill and eat others and how creatures defend themselves from being killed. What you see here, before your eyes, is how life is in our world. And we have it all here on our doorsteps, we just have to open our eyes to see it, and to understand it, to protect it. That is the true wonder."

Sometimes she would catch a butterfly in her net just so that people could have a close look at it, before letting it fly away unharmed. Sometimes she would ask the children to count the number of butterflies, which often ran into hundreds, trying, unsuccessfully, to make sure they didn't trample on any in the process. The children often used to try to catch the butterflies in their hand, thereby inadvertently injuring or killing them. Sometimes she would sit on the ground and ask the children to see how many different kinds of wildflowers they could find without picking them. And sometimes she would ask the children to be still and quiet and listen to a skylark singing overhead.

"I've visited this place all my life because it is so special. Not everyone who comes here realises that. But I hope you do after seeing the butterflies. This is their home, not my home or your home although we like to come and visit. It needs to be treated with respect in the same way as we would expect visitors to our homes to treat them with respect. To protect this place, and to stop all this destruction, we need your help to buy it."

"And if I could just add a few words?" said Joan, hesitatingly. "I find the butterflies so beautiful, I almost feel a spiritual connection with them, as if they represent something from beyond this world."

The people would applaud and dig into their pockets and Miss Crumble thanked them profusely from the bottom of her heart and handed out leaflets about the campaign, encouraging people to spread the word.

Miss Crumble would also give talks illustrated with slides about all the butterflies and the other wildlife that lived on the common to local groups in village halls and sometimes further afield. The slides were projected onto a screen, which was often just a white sheet with two wooden batons top and bottom hanging from the ceiling. Harriet stood by the screen and pointed at them with a walking stick. Joan accompanied her on these talks and operated the slide projector. There were times when the slides appeared on the screen upside down, and Joan became very flustered.

"I'm so sorry, I'm so sorry Harriet" she would say. Harriet would sigh deeply to express her disappointment. On one occasion Joan dropped the whole canister of slides whilst trying to load it into the machine. The slides made a clattering noise when they hit the wooden floor and ended up widely spread out in a jumble.

"Ladies and gentlemen there will be a ten minute delay whilst my accomplice rearranges the slides" said Miss Crumble in her matter-of-fact voice, with a slight tone of frustration.

"Oh Harriet, I do apologise. I don't know what happened. One minute I had the canister firmly in my hands but when I took the rubber band off out they all came, and look at the mess. Oh dear. I'm getting so cack-handed these days."

The talks were always very well received. Harriet would call out "Next slide please Joan" and Joan would get up from her chair to operate the slide projector, which would take a little while. "There we are Harriet, or have I missed one?" "That's fine, thank you Joan."

After the talks and over tea and biscuits, the chair of the group would give a vote of thanks to Harriet and Joan, and the treasurer of the group would present a cheque to the Save Our Common campaign. On more than one occasion the group had asked its members beforehand to make a craft item depicting the butterflies, and when Harriet was asked to judge the best one, she passed the responsibility over to Joan as she knew that was Joan's area of expertise.

The local press was given regular updates on the progress of the campaign. Once the target of the amount of money needed not just to buy the land but also to restore the ploughed up areas back to heath had been decided the paper printed a diagram like a thermometer every so often, showing how far along the scale the bid for funds had progressed. Each week the thermometer rose, sometimes fractionally, sometimes significantly as larger pledges of money were received. Jean Williams was responsible for all the behind-the-scenes administrative work, assisted by the Flight Commander and Joan who did the book-keeping. They met regularly and reviewed the progress, and came up with different ideas for raising funds. The Flight Commander had a brother who worked in the BBC, and he found that the BBC was keen to highlight and publicise out-of-the-ordinary stories from around Britain. This resulted in the BBC coming to the common to do some filming during the summer about the campaign, and the group decided that the best people to be filmed and interviewed by the BBC reporter were Luke and Harriet Crumble.

When the day for the filming arrived Luke came onto the common early to check his cattle, and then went to fetch Alina. He wanted her there not so much for some moral support, that would have been the case previously, but because he was proud of what the campaign was achieving and he wanted her to feel that, and to be proud of him. For the occasion Luke had borrowed a jacket from his father that was too big for him, with the sleeves coming over his hands.

"Quite the grown man now" remarked Alina.

Harriet Crumble arrived, dressed in flowing skirt, summer blouse, large straw hat and with butterfly net at the ready. Joan was with her, along with her small Yorkshire terrier called Ziggy.

"Have you thought about what you are going to say?" asked Joan.

"Of course I have Joan, but it does depend on what the questions the reporter wants to ask me" replied Harriet.

"I do hope your hat stays on, there's quite a breeze."

"The least of my concerns. I really don't know why you've brought Ziggy along with you. I just hope that you will keep her under control."

The BBC van arrived and the film crew got out. After all the preliminaries they finally set up the camera and started filming first the surviving parts of heathland on the common and then the potato fields, with the reporter doing a commentary based on what Luke had told him. Then the BBC wanted to film the butterflies. Miss Crumble stepped forward.

"Let me take you to where you can see them best."

Off they went, Miss Crumble striding out and the film crew struggling to keep up in her wake. When they arrived at a place where the pink heather was in full bloom the cameraman spoke.

"Crikey. The butterflies are all over the heather, there must be hundreds, if not thousands of the blighters."

"Blighters they are not" said Miss Crumble, raising her butterfly net as if to strike him with the wooden handle without actually doing so.

Once they had filmed the butterflies flying round the heather and taking nectar from the flowers the reporter interviewed Miss Crumble.

"So why are these butterflies worth saving?"

"Because they have become rare. This is their last sanctuary in this region, you will not find them within more than 50 miles of here. They used not to be rare, but so much of their heathland home has been lost to so-called progress or ploughing."

"But surely they are just butterflies, not worth anything, why should we care if they do disappear?"

"They are not just beautiful creatures that inspire us, they tell us something outside of ourselves and our daily human concerns. To turn the countryside into one big food factory diminishes us all. We share this world with thousands of different creatures whose lives are so different from our own, and, although we have the power to kill them off at will, we would all lose our connection with that sense of otherness. The butterflies, these beautiful and fragile creatures, are the standard-bearers, for, if they and the land that is their home are saved, all sorts of other creatures can flourish as well."

With that she caught a butterfly in her net, got it to sit on her finger and knelt down in front of the camera.

"Look how beautiful that is." The cameraman focussed on the butterfly, and then filming finished. Then Ziggy started jumping up at Miss Crumble and barking.

"Ziggy, Ziggy!" said Joan in a soft voice. "Oh dear. I'm so sorry. Oh why won't you behave!"

"It's all right madam, we've finished filming now" said the cameraman, who went up to Ziggy and started stroking her.

Next the reporter turned to Luke, and the cameraman started filming again.

"Now, young man, I understand that you have been at the forefront of trying to save the common. Is that right?"

Luke swallowed hard at first, fearing he wouldn't be able to get any words out. But then he began to talk, and the more he talked the easier he found it.

"Yes that's right. I live here and my Dad and I have a few cattle that graze the common, at least on those parts which are not being used to grow potatoes. All my life I have known this place, and it's my home, and I don't want to see it destroyed."

"But we need farmers to produce food for the country, especially in these times."

"I know that, but not this place, not the common. It means so much to so many people in so many different ways – commoners, walkers, people who like the wildlife, former RAF people. Even some local farmers feel that the common is not the right place to grow crops. We are going to save it, I am sure of that. But to do that we need people to donate money so that we can buy it"

"Thank you Luke. So, ladies and gentlemen, we have people here determined to save the common, and they reckon that the only way they can succeed is by purchasing it. But will they succeed? Only time will tell."

The BBC crew thanked everybody and left.

Car boot sales, jumble sales, coffee mornings, sponsored walks all helped to raise funds. Some events raised large amounts of money, and these included a concert organised by Jean Williams. She had two children, Jack aged 19 and Isobel aged 17. They were both talented musicians, with Jack playing the piano and Isobel the violin, and their mother persuaded them to give a concert in the local church as a fund-raiser. Sonatas by Bach and Mozart were followed by a piece that their mother had asked them to play, and which they had had to learn and practise many times over – The Lark Ascending by Ralph Vaughan Williams, in the version for piano and violin. The audience was completely hushed as the sound of the violin rose gently to fill the church. On and on it went, rising and falling, a violin on the wing. As the piece came to its gentle finish the audience remained quiet until someone clapped, and more and more people clapped until everyone clapped together, and Jack and Isobel held hands and smiled brightly as they acknowledged the applause. Everyone appreciated the connection of the piece to the skylarks on the common, and as they left the hall a huge amount was donated to the campaign, easily surpassing the amount raised by ticket sales.

It was, however, not all good fortune and happy days. Bill Westwood began to suffer from poor health, and complained that he wasn't able to do as much as he would have liked to help the campaign. It had been suggested that he appeared on camera with the BBC to help the campaign, but he said he was just not up to it. Soon afterwards he was confined to his bed and, despite the devoted attention of his friends and family, he died. Shortly before he died Luke had visited him and listened to him talk whilst sitting on his bedside.

"My days may be numbered, but at least we are on the road to saving the common. But is it the right road, is it the road we should have had to travel? The law should have protected the common. The law failed us dreadfully, and it not just that it needs changing as much as it needs to be properly followed through. There needs to be people around who can ensure the law is enforced, be they lawyers or anyone else. There will always be people around who will want to damage the common or the countryside in general in some way, and who is there to stop them? That's where you need to be thinking of putting your energy. You're an intelligent lad, and I know you care for the common, so think on that for what you might do with your life."

A memorial gathering took place on the common a few weeks later, with people coming from far and wide to remember him with words, poems, speeches, tributes, songs and beer. His horses and his wagon were driven onto the common for the last time. He left a huge legacy to the campaign, not only some of his savings but also an inspiration to others to value the common. Whilst it was initially seen as a setback for the campaign, it later became clear that his life and example would continue to benefit the common long after his death. More support flooded in.

The Flight Commander remained keen to see the sacrifice by members of the RAF killed on and around the airfield recognised, and he enlisted the help of another RAF base for a flypast low over the common. Former fighters and bombers, Spitfires and Hurricanes, Stirlings and Lancasters, all took part on a fine, cloudless afternoon. A crowd assembled on the common and the Flight Commander spoke to them through a loud hailer about the importance of erecting a memorial to those that had given their lives in the war. The planes roared their engines overhead as they flew overhead, with everyone applauding. The planes wheeled round and did a second pass before flying into the distance. Buckets were rattled and more money came into the campaign's coffers.

Even the local MP got involved, and he talked of putting forward a proposal for new laws to protect the countryside. People wondered if he was doing this just to try and secure more votes at the next general election or because he genuinely believed in the aims of the campaign. Although this did not in itself raise more money, it did raise the profile of the campaign. Luke spent some time with the MP discussing what was being proposed. He came to think that, although trying to buy the common was the right thing to do, maybe in the future when other sites are being threatened stronger and better legal safeguards would be more effective. So although his determination to see the common saved by being purchased was not diminished, it set him off on a train of thought about what might lie ahead for him in the future.

Luke himself thought long and hard about what he could do to raise funds. Eventually he decided to organise a sponsored run around the common. Each participant would have to run around the boundary of the common three times, and raise funds for the campaign by being sponsored by their families and friends. On the day of the Big Common Run over one hundred participants lined up, with Luke and Alina amongst them. Luke had asked his father to get things started, and he made a short speech.

"Years ago the people of the parish used to beat the bounds of the common every year, to ensure that nobody encroached onto the common. They went round the boundary of the common with sticks, hitting the ground. We may not be doing quite that today but by running round the boundaries we are marking what is and always will be the common, despite what has been going on here recently. Now then, if you're ready, on your marks, get set, go!" It was not a race, however, and off they went, some sprinting off whilst other did little more than walking pace. It took three hours for everyone to complete the run, but it raised far more than Luke had hoped for.

And then there was Alina. Luke asked her if there was anything she would like to do to help the campaign.

"You remember how I told you what Mr Hughes had done to me? And that he would have to suffer for it?"

"Well, yes. But what are you talking about? Are you going to hurt him in some way?"

"Of course."

"Ally, for goodness sake be careful. What are you going to do? I don't want to see you getting hurt again."

"Don't worry about me. But he needs to feel some pain and to be hurt where he would feel it most."

Luke was taken aback. "Surely you're not going to…"

"No, not there" replied Alina, smiling. "But close."

"So what are you going to do? Does it involve violence?"

"I'm going to knock on his door, that's all." As she said this she walked away from Luke.

Alina had been thinking about ways she could get back at Mr Hughes for a long time. Perhaps she should let the tyres down on his tractors. Or throw stones and break his windows. Or open some of his farm gates to let his animals out onto the roads. But none of these would really hurt him, merely inconvenience him for a short while. So she had come up with another idea.

Alina walked to Mr and Mrs Hughes' farmhouse and knocked at the front door. The door was opened by Mrs Hughes.

"Oh, it's you, the young Polish girl. What do you want now?"

"I want to tell you about your husband and how threw me to the ground one night in the woods, how he put his hand up my dress, and how he threatened to do more than that."

Mrs Hughes' face dropped, and she said nothing for a while before inviting Alina inside.

"My husband's out at the moment. Tell me what happened."

"I know that you will feel that I was wrong to try and eavesdrop on the meeting he and others had at the parish hall about ploughing up the common, but he found me out and chased me through the woods before he did what I told you. I don't want to keep repeating what he did because I get upset."

"And why are you telling me this?"

"He should be made to pay for what he did. It was wrong. He should have just given me a telling off and left it at that. I've never told anyone about what he did apart from Luke, but I could, I could tell a lot of people round here, I could make sure everyone round here knew about it. I don't think that you or he would like that to happen, would you?"

Mrs Hughes looked intently at Alina, and spoke in a serious tone of voice, indicating she had reason to believe what Alina had said.

"So what are you suggesting?"

"You know that there is a campaign to buy the common to restore it to how it used to be. You and he could make a contribution of say £200, maybe not directly but via someone else such as a solicitor."

"I think you should leave now. I shall speak to my husband about it."

A few days later Luke told Alina that a handsome donation of £200 had been received from a local solicitor. Alina told him of her conversation with Mrs Hughes.

"That's blackmail" said Luke.

"I don't care what you call it. They had no choice really as they knew their name and reputation would be damaged beyond repair. And I knew it would hurt him in his most hurtful place, his wallet. He would hate signing a cheque for that amount, it would really hurt. But it's the payment he had to make for hurting me. And he didn't just hurt me, he hurt the common too, so it's a way of making good two things."

Luke was speechless, until he said "Has it made you feel better, as that is the most important thing."

"To an extent. I think it will help. In effect he has admitted what he did was wrong, and that does help."

All the money raised, however, was still not sufficient not just for the purchase of the common and the associated fees, but also to do work to restore the damage done to the common by the ploughing. That was not until one very large anonymous donation was received. There was no way of telling who gave this money, which took the group over the line for the funds required, as it was received via a solicitor who explained that the donor did not want their name to be disclosed. Members of the group speculated as to who it might be – perhaps the rector had given the money as a penance, maybe the local member of the aristocracy, Sir Geoffrey, had donated the money as it was thought he could well afford it, or maybe another member of the group had decided to donate it without liking to let the others know. However the important thing was that the target had been reached.

Luke was now sixteen years old and it was time for him to think about what he was going to do in the future. He had already decided to stay on at school to take exams in order to get a university place.

When it came to deciding which subject he would like to study at university he spoke to his aunt Jean about what the local MP had said to him concerning a change in the law to offer the countryside greater protection, as this line of thought had occupied him for several weeks since saw Bill Westwood for the last time.

"I can see that buying the common is the only way to save it in reality. But should it be like this? The common is not and should not be the only place where the wildlife can flourish and where people can enjoy the peace and tranquillity of the countryside. You can't save the whole countryside by buying it all, that's clearly ridiculous. It just needs protecting better, especially those areas that are farmed. Farming does not have to wipe out all the wildlife, and farmers should be welcoming people to enjoy the countryside rather than telling them to clear off."

"You have been giving this a lot of thought, I can see."

"My teachers tell me that I can get a place at university if I study hard enough. To be honest, all that has been going on with the common has been something of a distraction from my school work, but I know I can make up the lost ground. I am determined to do that. What do you think? You know me as well as anyone."

"That sort of determination was not present in you just a few months ago. How you've changed. It won't be easy, not just the study you will have to put in, long evenings at the kitchen table reading and writing, but also because universities only tend to take the children of professional people. But if you have the faith in yourself, a new found faith, you certainly can do it. But tell me now about you and your father. Do you talk much about your mother, or even about the pilot?"

"It's not easy for him, and perhaps it's easier for me in a way. Visiting her grave was really hard for him, he just completely filled up. In his own way he was so fond of her. She brought happiness into his life, yet also pain when she started seeing the pilot. He put some flowers on the grave, flowers he had gathered from the common, and then bent down on his knees and began to weep. I tried to comfort him, but the tears kept coming. After he had wiped them away he told me how much he loved her, how he felt that he was not really worthy of marrying such a beautiful, intelligent and kind woman, and how he felt I had inherited many of her characteristics. He then got to his feet and hugged me, and the tears flowed again. It was all a bit weird to be honest, as I had never seen him like that before, ever, although I am sure it helped him. We've been back since then to tidy up the grave and we planted some spring bulbs, and he seemed to cope with that much better. He's always been a practical man, always wanting to be occupied doing something rather than talking, and I suppose that was easier for him than the first time we went. But I do think that the first time was really important for him. Generally now he just seems a much more relaxed person, as if he has managed to express something he has been holding inside for a long, long time has finally come out. Not been at all easy for him though."

"But what about you, it can't have been straightforward for you either."

"I know. But after I had found out about her life at the end, and about her and the pilot, it made me feel much more able to remember her, to want to remember her as the kind and loving person she was rather than just push her memory into the background. I'm proud to be her son, and if people like my dad see things in me that they saw in her, then that makes me feel even prouder. And what I do in life will always be with her by my side. In a way, going through all of that has enabled me to fight to save the common, as the two things - facing up to the past and dealing with the present - have gone hand in hand."

"And I'm proud of you, how you've dealt with all of this. I too see my sister in you. You've done a lot of growing up in the last few months, like hacking your way through a dark jungle and finally arriving at a sunlit clearing. Come, let me kiss you."

And they kissed each other on the cheek.

It was summer when the full amount needed had been raised. Conveyancing was completed, and the day of the grand celebration had arrived. Hundreds of people came onto the common. Marquees were put up, sandwiches, pies and cakes were provided, speeches were made, and a huge ribbon was placed across one of the ways onto the common. Harriet Crumble, George Porter, Jean Williams and Luke all held onto a large pair of scissors as the ribbon was cut.

9.

A Stranger

Everyone knew, however, that restoring the areas that had been sprayed with chemicals, ploughed, manured and fertilised would not be straightforward. Luke would recall more of the words of Bill Westwood had said shortly before he died: "All that chicken shit, all those chemicals, all that fertiliser, you're going to get nothing but weeds, docks and thistles. God knows what you can do about it, how you can get it back to the poor soils heathland needs? You'll have to get some expert involved, someone who knows, because I haven't got a clue." And so Luke and the rest of the campaign group made sure someone with the knowledge and experience was hired to advise everyone on how best to restore the common. The group was also keen to ensure that the Flight Commander would have something to mark the sacrifice made by the pilots and aircrew, and so it was agreed that the old control tower would be restored as their lasting memorial. One chapter in the life of the common closed and another was about to begin.

The day after the grand opening Luke went round to Alina's house.

"Here's the hero" said Alina's father as he opened the door and invited Luke inside.

"I'm no hero, just part of a team" he replied as they walked through into the kitchen.

Alina's mother had just baked some cakes.

"You've timed that just perfect, I've just got to put the toppings on then you can help yourself. Come here young man." And with those words she put her arms around Luke and gave him a big kiss on both cheeks.

"Mum!" Alina had just entered the room. "That's so just not right."

All four of them sat down to tea and cakes, and talked about the events of the previous day. Then Luke told Alina to get her coat as they were going out onto the common.

The marquees were being taken down. Pieces of bunting were flapping around the common, caught in bushes. The atmosphere was one of the morning after the night before. Luke and Alina sat down on the fallen oak tree trunk where they had sat and talked many times previously.

"So what are you going to do next" asked Alina.

"I've got a lot to do. I can't be spending the rest of my life here on the common, trying to put back to heathland all the parts that were ploughed up. It's more a case of one part of my life finishes, and perhaps another will be starting soon. The headteacher at school says I've still got a good chance of getting to university if I put the work in."

"You, at university?"

"It's what I want, and I'm prepared to put the effort in."

"But what about the common? And what about your cattle?"

"The money that's been raised will pay for someone else to come in and make sure the common is properly restored and looked after. Do I want to spend the rest of my life herding a few cattle in all weathers? Bill Westwood knew how hard that life is."

"And what do you want to study at university, pray?"

"Law."

"You, Luke, want to be a lawyer?" said Alina, somewhat incredulously.

"What happened here, with the common being disrespected, should never have happened. And it should never have been necessary for the campaign group to buy the common, as it should have been protected by laws. It's something Bill Westwood said to me just before he died. Laws will be coming in to stop that sort of thing from happening again, that's been one good thing that's come out of all this, new laws to protect our countryside. Those laws will need drafting, and they will need to be enforced, otherwise they will be ignored. That's what I want to be part of, protecting our countryside from people who want to destroy it."

A pause.

"So, what happened to that shy, indecisive young lad who picked up a pen belonging to a pilot?" asked Alina, quietly.

"A lot happened. Can't really believe it did all happen."

"It changed you. You were always a good lad, but you came to know that what you felt deep inside you was right, and that gave you more belief in yourself. And perhaps I was wrong to criticise you as much as I did – I was pretty tough with you at times, more so than I should have been I think."

"It's OK, it didn't do any harm really. Perhaps I needed that, as I saw myself too much as a victim. But it is weird to hear you of all people expressing some doubt about yourself, what you did and said, maybe even some remorse. Not really like you at all."

"Maybe not. Luke, I'm truly sorry if I hurt you. A more confident Luke yes, but I don't want you to lose your gentler and more sensitive side."

Silence. Luke reached out with his hand and held Alina's hand in his. Before, she would have instantly withdrawn her hand and asked him what on earth he was doing, but not now. They were holding hands tenderly, affectionately. She looked down, and then looked up to meet Luke's eyes. Luke could see that tears were forming in her eyes.

"I suppose I've got to go. My Mum needs some help in the house." Her voice was breaking as she said these words, and soon she was gone.

Luke stayed sitting on the oak tree, thinking about everything, the common, his father, Alina, Bill Westwood,

Harriet Crumble. Minutes passed. He felt something on his shoulder. He turned his head and saw a hand in a black leather glove resting on his shoulder. He gave a sudden gasp. He turned round and saw a woman standing there, wearing a dark tweed coat, a hat, spectacles, with a handbag over her arm and a stern expression on her face.

"You're Luke, aren't you" she said, in a Scottish accent.

Yes, I'm Luke, but I don't think I know who you are" replied Luke, his voice shaking.

The woman walked round the fallen tree and sat next to him.

"I recognised you from seeing you on the BBC television. My husband was killed here in the war when his plane crashed. He was badly burnt in the fire that followed, and died a day later in hospital."

"Flight Lieutenant Jim Craig?"

"Aye. And I'm his widow." Luke remembered that the Flight Commander had told him that the pilot was Scottish, and recognised from her accent that his widow was Scottish too.

"I saw him on the night of the crash."

"He was a very brave man, and I still miss him, every day."

Luke took the fountain pen from his pocket. "I found this sometime after the crash. It was his, I think, and you'd better have it now", and he gave it to the woman. She took it and gently held it in her fingers, turning it round to read the inscription of his name.

"I gave it to him, and had it engraved with his name. He had to be careful not to take it with him when he was flying over enemy territory, but he could have it with him here. He had beautiful writing, so it was fitting that he had a fine pen." With that she opened the metal clasp on her handbag and took out a postcard.

"This was the last thing he wrote to me, a postcard of this place. I've always kept it with me." She handed it to Luke. He could see that on the front was a photograph of the heather in full flower on the common. He turned it over and spoke the words that the pilot had written with the fountain pen.

"Such a beautiful heath, so good to walk here in the few moments of peace. Sad to think what may happen to a place like this when this war's over. Someone will probably come along and plough it all up. Love, Jim."

"He came to love this place. He was a brave airman and flew many missions over enemy territory before he started training other pilots. But he was a reluctant fighter, as he was a man of peace, who loved nothing more than a walk in unspoilt countryside. We used to go for many such walks, arm in arm. He would point out to me the names of all the birds. He also spent much of his time campaigning to protect the wildlife back home in Scotland. He would often say to me that we are just one species and that all other creatures have a right to a home far away from our meddling and interference."

Luke smiled and then spoke. "He could see what was going to happen here, more than any of us. He knew that it would be ploughed up, that's incredible." He thought again of the night when the plane had crashed and how the pilot ran towards him, looking at him as if to tell him something, before the pilot fell to the ground covered in flames. And he also thought about the pilot's grave and how flowers had been laid there.

"I saw you on the television and heard about the campaign to save this place. That's why I made a donation to help the campaign. I did it in memory of my husband. I'd like to think that he played a part in saving the common."

"So it was you who gave that big sum of money?"

"It was both of us, me and my husband."

Luke went to hand the postcard back to her.

"No, you keep it. And the pen too. I am not well, and have not much time left now. I so wanted to see this place again before I go, and to meet you." She handed the pen back to Luke. "They belong together."

Luke could see that she was fighting back her tears, but soon she got up and walked away, leaving Luke sitting alone clutching the pen and the postcard in the sunshine on the common.

Background to the Book

In 2006 the UK charity Butterfly Conservation purchased the western half of Prees Heath Common in Shropshire from an offshore company, following a campaign stretching back to the 1980s. The Common provides the last remaining sanctuary in the Midlands for the Silver-studded Blue butterfly. Much of the site had been in arable cultivation for around 40 years, thereby destroying the heathland habitat that had been looked after by the Commoners for centuries, and prior to that it was a World War Two RAF airfield. The campaign to save the Common, which had also been threatened with sand and gravel extraction, was supported by many groups including the Commoners, the West Midlands Branch of Butterfly Conservation, Shropshire Wildlife Trust and local residents. Together with public donations from around the country following a national appeal, a grant for the purchase and restoration of this half of the Common was secured from GrantScape, a Landfill Tax Environmental Body. I was appointed Prees Heath Officer in 2006 to restore the site, and since my retirement in 2016 I continue as Volunteer Warden.

Although the book is loosely based on what happened at Prees Heath Common several years ago, it is a work of fiction. All royalties from the book's publication will go to Butterfly Conservation for the continued restoration of Prees Heath Common. To learn more about how you can support the work of Butterfly Conservation please visit:

www.butterfly-conservation.org

Butterfly Conservation
Saving butterflies, moths and our environment

BV - #0023 - 291019 - C0 - 216/140/12 - PB - 9781912419883